HOME SHATTERED

HOME SHATTERED

PC NOTTINGHAM

Published By: The Little Horsemen an imprint of 4 Horsemen Publications, Inc.

The Little Horsemen Publications
℅ 4 Horsemen Publications, Inc.
PO Box 419
Sylva, NC 28779
4horsemenpublications.com
info@4horsemenpublications.com

Cover Illustration by Oxford
Cover Typography and Typesetting by Autumn Skye
Edited by Tabitha Saletri

Library of Congress Control Number: 2025943866

Paperback ISBN-13: 979-8-8232-0976-2
Hardcover ISBN-13: 979-8-8232-0977-9
Audiobook ISBN-13: 979-8-8232-0979-3
Ebook ISBN-13: 979-8-8232-0978-6

DEDICATION

This series is dedicated to all of the children caught in the crossfire of adults who can't put aside their differences, especially to all the people whose homes have been shattered by war.

TABLE OF CONTENTS

ACKNOWLEDGMENTS

There are so many amazing people to thank for their support in bringing this series from a crazy idea into your hands: all of the wonderful people at 4HP who took a chance on me, Monique Bucheger, N.C. Scrimgeour, D. Everett Thomas, KC Woodruff, Kathrin Spinnler, Jaci Lunera, Martha Flick, Alex Bree, Elise Edmonds, Nico Vincenty, Hanna Day, Loren Huxley, Mick Vernant, Karim Ragab, N.E. White, AJ Braun, Tiffany O'Haro, and the whole Cru at the Radio Freewrite podcast (WebEater, Krispy, Murph, The Lotus, and Spud). They're all amazing creators and worth checking out!

1

JAB

- Divine Poetics

Each bob of the sailing cog signaled the same thing to Jab: he'd never ventured so far from home. Yet with his twin brother Sanu beside him, he also had never been closer to home, even though their personalities were chafing again. Three months ago, their parents had died. Not even a day later, Jab believed Sanu had died and Sanu believed the same about Jab. Soldiers on opposite sides of a battle saved each brother.

Where the others on this ship may have seen blue waves, when Jab stared at the sea, he saw the flames again, ripping through the grass on the hill where he'd played. When that battle erupted outside their hometown, the brothers weren't the only ones divided.

All the ruckus of the sailors around him loading the boats couldn't drown out that night's screams ringing in Jab's head.

The knight who'd saved Sanu sailed with them today. Yet the scout who'd saved Jab, the one who'd been like a brother to him in the following weeks, perished. While Sanu's guardian was on the losing side and Jab's victorious, that scout died defending Jab in the Holy City. Jab was glad to be reunited with his true brother but losing his savior left him hollow.

Jab tore his eyes from the horizon's imagined flames and sighed. He lifted his brown, bushy tail and dabbed at his eyes.

Sanu elbowed him. "I thought your time training to be a scout would've toughened you up. Are you thinking about a girl, or wishing you could climb a tree?"

From behind, the knight slapped his beaver tail against the wooden ship deck. "Squirrels love trees." Sir Brouglas's accent was thick and betrayed an unfamiliarity with their language. "That's why he cries? Doesn't like the ocean?"

"No," Jab said to both. "It's the ocean water. I can't believe how much salt is in my fur. It's getting in my eyes."

Sanu arched an eyebrow and lowered his voice. "What's wrong?"

"You wouldn't understand."

Sanu folded his arms. "Fine. After a week at sea, I thought you'd be able to talk to me about stuff again."

Jab *had* answered all of Sanu's questions regarding his time last month with Nasalid the Liberator since they departed, but he remembered their promise to each other. He wouldn't snap at him. "You're right. We agreed to get along at Mom and Dad's funeral." Jab forced a smile. "I'm glad that I was wrong, but I guess it's still weird knowing you're alive."

"Well, I do understand *that*," Sanu said.

A hamster sailor behind them shouted something in Frenglese, and the beaver knight retorted while pointing at Sanu.

Forcing a chuckle, Sanu translated. "He said we could clean the deck if we have time to stand around and talk, and Sir Brouglas said I need to spar with him."

The beaver knight chortled. "Heard that, I did!"

"Now come on." Sanu tapped Dad's scimitar attached to his belt. "Show me some moves the scout taught you. I want to beat Sir Brouglas."

Seeing Sir Brouglas as anything other than a foreigner who occupied the Holy City proved difficult for Jab. Some part of him resented the beaver for what he represented, but seeing how kind he was, Jab forced himself to look past that. Without worrying about his different religion or culture, Brouglas had saved Sanu's life, even if he hadn't saved Jab from chores on the boat.

Watching Brouglas's approving smile as Sanu waved his scimitar made Jab want to forget the last few months and move forward.

Someone shouted from the crow's nest in Frenglese, making Sanu and Sir Brouglas stop. Jab tried to be more proud than jealous that his brother had picked up some of their language in his time with them.

Sanu rushed back to the deck's edge. "He spotted land!"

Jab squinted at the faint shoreline. He couldn't do much to forget the last few months anymore now that they'd reached their destination, the whole point of this journey.

They had a prisoner to deliver, along with news about the Holy City.

"Are you going to tell her?" Jab asked. "Should Brouglas?"

Sanu cocked a grin. "Let's do it together. I want to see the look on that mole rat's face when she realizes it's time for her to pay for her crimes."

Sir Brouglas slapped his tail against the deck, stealing their attention. "We don't talk bad about rodents we no like. She is still powerful until King Hedgry punishes her. Join me."

Jab nodded, wondering how the beaver could stick up for Lady Marjitay. When the Holy City fell to the Liberator last month, she'd refused to surrender at first, killing the holy man she was supposed to share power with. Some part of Jab wished she'd stand trial for her real crime of occupying the Holy City instead of only the unjust killing of one rodent. As he followed Brouglas below deck, the ship felt less steady, with the sailors bouncing around, shouting their joy at seeing home.

Not knowing Frenglese as well as Sanu made Jab feel even more alone. Disliking the foul Lady Marjitay was the only true unifier among the entire crew.

While the ship was too small for a proper prison, the captain had kept the mole rat holed up in a cabin, and a guard at the door at all times. Without her famous crossbow, Jab didn't see how she was a threat to anyone, but he appreciated how the captain had kept his word to the Liberator.

Sir Brouglas waved to the guard and exchanged quick pleasantries.

Sanu whispered to Jab, "He's telling him we spotted land and we're going to tell Lady Marjitay."

Jab had guessed that himself, but didn't want to insult his brother. It took thinking the other was dead to get them to be nice to each other and he had already tested that today.

The guard, an old porcupine, smiled at the boys and stepped aside, opening the door for them. The supply room allowed a cone of light from a porthole, illuminating the storage barrels and the prisoner.

The mole rat inside still wore her fineries, since she'd been marched directly onto this ship without any of her belongings. The sea's salt and stench had turned them a dull, slimy gray, which was a pleasant sight compared to her grimace.

"Brouglas," she hissed. Jab didn't need a translator for the name or the hate dripping between her protruding teeth.

The beaver replied, and Sanu translated. "He told her we spotted land, and she's about to face trial for murdering a Sapling in King Hedgry's court by tomorrow."

"She already knows that," Jab whispered.

"I think it's their law or something," Sanu replied. "Brouglas also served her, so he also has to follow a law where he tells her stuff, I think."

Lady Marjitay snorted something and tossed her head.

"She told him she'd do it again and that he's a disgrace," Sanu translated.

Jab shook his head. She lived up to the nickname of the Honking Goose. The gestures she made with her paws and her tone transcended every language barrier. She was threatening the three of them. Jab's faith taught that no rodents were truly bad, but politicians like her made him doubt.

2

SANU

Salutations to you all. Accept the news that the Holy City has surrendered. The Goose Clan is hereby expelled, and I release Lady Marjitay to you. On my honor, unarmed Sprouter pilgrims will be welcomed into Zelzaytun. My solemn wish is to end the bloodshed over holy ground.

- Excerpt from Nasalid the Liberator's message to the Frenglese kings.

As the shoreline solidified, Sanu could barely contain himself. After the meeting with Lady Marjitay, fresh air felt great. Sanu's bare hindpaws slapped against the deck and he cringed, realizing he should've stopped to pray with his brother. He hadn't had an opportunity to do so over the last few months, except when he finally broke the holy fast after the city surrendered. Jab had spent all that time with Sanu's hero, Nasalid the Liberator.

This critical message was for King Hedgry, the strongest in the Frenglese islands. His might kept the kings on other islands from fighting each other, so sending Nasalid's message of peace to him made the most sense.

But as a Grovekeeper who was passably bilingual and had an understanding of the Sprouters, Sanu was trusted with a copy of the message, Sir Brouglas with another, and one of Nasalid's soldiers with the third. But that soldier never wanted to show Sanu any sword fighting moves, so he wasn't as impressive. Sanu wished the scout Jab kept mentioning had survived. *He* would've shown Sanu a thing or two. All Sanu wanted to do was train with deadly weapons.

How unreasonable was that for a twelve-year old?

"Watch out," a familiar squirrel called. It was Yagub, Sir Brouglas's squire. He could've been Sanu and Jab's older brother, for how he looked and sounded. He was from Qawar island like them, even though he belonged to the Sprouter religion like Brouglas. He'd been Sanu's main language tutor and helped Brouglas learn some phrases of their language.

"I *am* watching out," Sanu replied.

Yagub carried a wooden crate and motioned at another behind him. "How about you make yourself useful? I'd ask your brother, but he's conveniently occupied right now."

Jab was kneeling near the ship's railing, saying his morning prayers.

Sanu glowered at Yagub. "He's actually doing what he's supposed to do." He debated stepping on Yagub's tail, but decided against it. *Why was Yagub so testy?* This should be exciting for Yagub, getting to meet Sprouter royalty.

Sanu grabbed the crate, and something rattled around inside. He hoped it was arrows or crossbow bolts. It would be good to get as many of those off Qawar as possible. As he shifted his weight to balance the heavy crate, he guessed it might also be holy objects Nasalid was returning as a sign of good faith to the Frenglese. Sanu didn't know much about these Sprouters, even after his time with them, but he did know they liked their artwork and their sacred thingamabobs.

Sanu wondered if Jab would laugh or frown at Sanu calling them thingamabobs, but decided against trying the joke on him. Nobody seemed to be in a good mood today.

A sailor stood on the railing, ripped off his shirt, and swung it around in a circle, cheering for the approaching land.

Well, nobody close to Sanu was in a good mood.

Along the shoreline were rows of stone buildings, all bigger than the ones in his hometown of Rattin and about the same size as the ones in the Holy City. Yet these didn't have the aura of history and holiness pulsing through them. He spotted some Gnaverwood trees in the distance, but those didn't rise as high as the colossal one in the center of the Holy City, the central object of worship for both the Sprouters' faith and his own, Grovekeeping.

Maybe Sanu *had* learned something in his time with them, though he would've rather learned how to shoot a crossbow and swing a scimitar.

Sir Brouglas stomped up behind Sanu, escorting Lady Marjitay with a guard. Seeing her in shackles did bring a twinge of satisfaction, but it wouldn't bring back his parents. It wouldn't bring back the Sapling she'd murdered. For a brief second, Sanu debated tackling her, making her fall overboard.

A few feet away, Jab rose from his prayer position, and Sanu's cheeks flushed. Seeing his faithful brother reminded Sanu that the All-Planter probably had rules about throwing rodents over the side of ships.

Yagub and Sanu set their crates down by the loading plank and Yagub nudged Sanu. "This is the first news they're getting that Olihort was under siege and that she was defeated. Expect people to be surprised."

Jab materialized beside them and huffed. "Olihort?"

Sanu measured his brother's expression. Olihort was what the Sprouters called the Holy City.

"Lots of places have two names." Yagub inclined his head. "Force of habit. ZelZaytun." Hearing the Grovekeeper name didn't do much for Sanu anymore, but it did seem to lift Jab's spirits.

As the cog ship slowed, approaching the dock, some knights carrying flags with a hawk and rake design came out. Yagub pointed at them.

"Those are King Hedgry's banners. He's not more important than the other Kings in Freng, but he does have the strongest army and the scariest reputation."

"I thought that was the Ridgerd guy I keep hearing about," Sanu said.

Yagub placed his tail over Sanu's shoulders. "Prince Ridgerd is *why* King Hedgry has that reputation."

"But why are they all wearing black?" Jab asked. "Is that normal for knights in Freng?"

"Not unless there's been a funeral," Yagub said.

A brassy horn sounding pulled Sanu's attention to the city streets. Some big procession was happening. Sir Brouglas came to the sailing cog's unloading plank, Lady Marjitay in tow.

"Who died?" Brouglas and the ship's captain glanced at each other, then the captain signaled to the welcoming group below.

"We come with news, but it seems you have some as well," the captain shouted.

Jab tiptoed to Sanu's side. "What're they saying?"

The banner carrier called back up. "You'll meet with King Ridgerd when he is ready. We have finished burying the late King Hedgry in the All-Planter's mercy."

Sanu nudged Jab and translated. "The king we were supposed to meet just died, so we've got to meet this King Ridgerd instead."

"Ridgerd," Jab repeated. "I've heard about him. Nasalid and his advisers talked about him a few times." Jab's tone darkened. "He's a vicious fighter."

Sanu wondered what it would be like for a military man to have to stop his campaigns and come home to rule instead. He couldn't imagine someone like Sir Brouglas stepping away from the military.

As the captain, Brouglas, and Lady Marjitay departed, Sanu met his brother's gaze. "I'm sorry I didn't pray with you before. I hope you didn't think it was because I didn't care. I was afraid to pray around some of the Sprouters, and I got out of the habit. Please remind me and I promise I will."

Surprised, Jab cocked his head.

Praying hadn't become important to Sanu until he believed Jab had died. Being a good Grovekeeper, especially in the presence of Sprouters, had been something Sanu wanted to do to honor Jab's memory, which felt weird now.

"I didn't really think about it," Jab said. "And I guess I was a little embarrassed to pray with you, because I didn't want you to notice that I lost Mom's prayer rock."

Dad's scimitar felt heavy on Sanu's belt. They each only had one thing to remind them of their parents. "I'm sorry, Jab."

"Don't be," Jab said. "It actually stopped one of those devilbeak weapons from killing me during the ZelZaytun siege. I didn't lose it as much as it got broken in a fight."

Sanu's jaw dropped. His brother had fought someone who used a devilbeak, the coolest weapon in the Great Sea. He was about to say he was jealous, but closed his mouth upon noticing the trauma in his twin's eyes and wiggling whiskers. "Um, I think it's time for us to disembark."

Sanu bent to pick up his crate, and Jab helped him. They descended the plank, trailing Yagub. Nasalid's soldier marched behind them. The rodents who greeted them sported Sprouter symbols on their clothing: the rake of Ganan the Gardener, the first Sprouter. The hawk on the late King Hedgry's banner was stylistically perched on one, and he much preferred that to the cross-bow-wielding goose on Lady Marjitay's banner.

He felt pretty cultured, appreciating and critiquing art in his head, and had a certain girl back in ZelZaytun in mind he wished he could tell.

Placing the crate on the wooden dock, Sanu stiffened and pushed the thought of girls from his mind. Jab had done a good job keeping quiet about his crush back home, so he should do the same. Besides, the hamster who he definitely only liked as a friend was doing important work for Nasalid back in the Holy City. She was a Sapling now, which Sanu knew was a big deal, he just couldn't remember exactly what it meant.

But he for sure wished she was here right now, since things had become more complicated.

3

JAB

- Raticenna's Collected Sermons.

Jab shuddered; Nasalid hadn't prepared Jab and Sanu for a dead king.

Their mission was to deliver Nasalid's message to King Hedgry and the Sapling who lived on this island. As the biggest Frenglese island closest to Qawar, this had been the springboard for the invasions back when Jab's grandparents were alive, if the stories were true. That fact, along with King Hedgry's power, made this the best choice for Nasalid to send his message. Now, with a dead monarch, this foreign city was the last place in the world Jab wanted to be.

Leaving the sailing cog, Jab and Sanu followed the procession toward the city's center, protected by banner carriers. The *clop-clop-clop* of horses' hooves and the creaking wheels of Lady Marjitay's prisoner cart punctuated the dull buzz around the city.

"What kinds of rodents live in the Frenglese islands?" Sanu asked.

"I don't even know how many islands there are."

Sanu shrugged. "Well, we know they're all Sprouters, and you, me, and Sergeant Jandi are the only Grovekeepers for miles."

Onlookers peered at them from bakeries, smithies, little shops, and homes. Where ZelZaytun city's main scents were cinnamon and olives, the sewage stench overtook any pleasant confection and food smells.

And with each step, Jab was even farther from home.

He measured the expressions of the hamsters and porcupines in the street, their eyes fixed on Lady Marjitay. He wondered how many people knew who she was, or if the dirty noble's clothes drew their attention. Either way, the whispers in a language he didn't know added to Jab's feeling of trespassing. He tempted fate and whispered to Nasalid's sergeant who had joined them. The bilingual squirrel was a rodent of few words, and had been indifferent to the brothers on the trip.

"Hey, Jandi, do you still have your copy of the message?" Jab worried that they wouldn't accept the message from a kid.

"Of course I do," Jandi retorted. "Eyes front. Nasalid proclaimed peace, but we are in enemy lands."

"Yeah," Sanu said. "This is an unsafe city in hostile territory, and we came at a confusing time for them."

The wood houses and shops gave way to stony towers, and they reached a place of worship. Jab couldn't tell by the size and the amount of stained glass if this was a Gananhall or a Gananshed, but he imagined a city of this size would have one Gananhall and several smaller Ganansheds like in ZelZaytun, if he remembered the difference between them correctly. One was for the whole region, and the other was for neighborhoods.

An old porcupine stood outside, and the unthinkable lay in his paws: a gold bowl, holding a single olive. It wasn't a grand one from the sacred Gnaverwood tree on Qawar island, but a small replacement, an imitation. Other rodents gathered around this tiny fruit on bended knees.

Jab's eyes widened. Sprouters used olives in their worship practices? Olives to eat during their services and olive oil for use in blessing boggled the mind. Back in ZelZaytun, the Sprouters profaned the holy tree by using its olives, but these must have come from local trees. ZelZaytun's tree was sacred to them too, wasn't it? How could Sprouters casually replace the beauty of the real thing?

But as Jab continued walking, he noticed everyone in the party except himself, Sanu, and Jandi bowed to the porcupine and the olive in his paw.

If this tiny olive was a holy thing to them, maybe they wanted it to be a part of their everyday life. Back home on Qawar, the holy island, the olive Gnaverwood tree could be part of their daily life. Maybe planting these imitations was as close as Sprouters could get.

Jab's mouth dried. He didn't want to look down on them for their practices that seemed strange to him. Maybe strange wasn't even the right word.

Different.

Though a tickle in his conscience reminded him that the similarities were more important.

One Sprouter in their group didn't acknowledge the porcupine: Lady Marjitay. She remained as aloof as ever. Jab wondered if the image of Ganan's rake on her clothing and coat of arms meant as much to her as the goose symbol.

As they passed the holy Gananhall building, the stony towers coalesced into a fortified wall. They'd reached a castle, or maybe they'd been in one the whole time and this was the central keep. A troop of guards wielding devilbeaks stood at attention before the wrought iron gate. The weapon sent a shiver up Jab's spine, remembering his confrontation with Lady Marjitay's adviser, the foul man who would've killed Jab had it not been for Mom's prayer rock.

The weapon, a long polearm, held a combination of a spearpoint, a hammer, and a pickax, giving it the shape of a hook-beaked bird's head. How Sanu could drool over it was a mystery. Jab had seen their destructive power firstpaw.

The guards called for the opening of the gate and the heavy latticework iron was raised. As the gate rose over Jab's head, he noticed a hawk design carved into it, resembling the symbol on the banner carriers escorting them.

Sir Brouglas looked over his shoulder at Sanu and Jab. "Welcome to Castle Graganet, home of lemon-dairy kings."

The brothers snickered. "Legendary," Sanu corrected.

"That was close," Jab added. "Your Qawari is getting better. You all need to teach me Frenglese."

"His Qawari is not getting better," Yagub chortled.

Sanu responded in Frenglese, and the ship captain chuckled, leaving Jab out.

Behind them, Jandi scoffed. "Get us in front of the king, beaver."

Jab wondered why Jandi acted like such a nut shell. He got to carry a message from Nasalid the Liberator. He couldn't think of a higher honor than to be trusted with such a task. It was one of three copies, but still, an honor was an honor.

On the other side of the gate, Sir Brouglas spoke with a soldier who had a few stripes on his outer tunic covering his armor, which Jab guessed meant he was some kind of officer. The beaver pointed to Lady Marjitay, and then to the case on his belt which held Nasalid's message, and the similar cases carried by Sanu and Jandi. Jandi folded his arms.

Lady Marjitay hissed something, and Jab didn't need his brother to translate to know it was hateful.

Jab scrunched his nose and tugged on Sanu's sleeve. "Could you tell them that Nasalid would be sad to hear about their king's death?"

Sanu pulled his arm away and glowered. "Don't cause a scene."

Backing away, Jab noticed the hurt in Sanu's eyes. This was twice Jab had unintentionally embarrassed Sanu. He should've been proud of his brother for learning another language in a short time, but instead he was screwing everything up.

Everyone's eyes bored into him—even the foul mole rat's.

SANU

*- General Ironseed's third
letter to the ruling council*

Sanu stifled his rage at his brother. After
the time Sanu had spent, maybe wasted,
lamenting a dead twin who was really alive, he
had to remember that Jab had done the same.
Jab had learned to ask Nasalid's soldiers for help
in the last few months, and it wasn't like Sanu
had been the most helpful twin before they were
separated at the battle of Rattin and before their
parents had died. Everyone assumed that twin
brothers were best friends automatically, but

Sanu had always wondered if they were born on different islands to different parents.

And seeing how Jab didn't trust him at this moment, that old theory resurfaced.

"If you're done drawing attention to yourself," Sanu mumbled to Jab, "they're waving us into the main keep."

"Oh, right," Jab said, whiskers drooping. "Nasalid was just so compassionate, and I think these Frengs should know."

"He was ruthless when he was younger and fighting for his uncle. Now he's too compassionate," Jandi mumbled.

Yagub glanced over his shoulder at them. "Don't worry. They'll know. He could've sent a head instead of a prisoner."

Sanu glanced up at the mole rat everyone called the Honking Goose and wondered if that would've been the better choice, but he swallowed that thought down. If Nasalid had treated her like a common criminal, it would've caused a bigger problem here, even if she was a murderer.

The Sapling she'd killed was a good rodent, and Sanu wished more Sprouters were like him. Sanu had witnessed his kindness firstpaw.

The keep's entrance had a long purple carpet ascending a staircase. The whole interior was cut from gray stone, livened up by artwork and tapestries along the walls, illuminated by stained-glass windows and torches. While the keep's exterior was gray, the inside was a rainbow.

Jab and the others ascended a wide curling staircase, and Lady Marjitay was removed from her prisoner cart to march beside Brouglas.

Jab elbowed Sanu. "What do you think these Sprouters will be like?"

"Nice, I hope. More like Brouglas than Marjitay."

The beaver smirked. "She is still a lady, even though criminal."

Sanu shook his head. There was nothing "noble" about her. Now, back in ZelZaytun, there was a certain hamster girl who was quite noble. Not that Sanu was still thinking about her. But he did wonder if she was thinking about him. She had more important things to do though. And Sanu technically did too.

A set of wide double doors loomed before them, and two guards wielding devilbeaks opened them. Sanu wanted to reach out and touch one of their weapons for the sake of having a cool story, but decided against it, having just gotten mad at Jab for making a scene, so he settled for letting his tail brush against the left guard's weapon. While the action was pointless because the steel weapon just felt like steel, it was also awesome and Sanu wanted a chance to do that again on their way out.

Inside, the long carpet extended to a throne on a dais, but the seat was barely visible because of the giant hamster sitting upon it.

The hamster stood, dwarfing everyone else in the room.

His muscles showed through his tunic, and he looked like he could have hurled the throne across the room with little effort. To his left, in a neat pile on a high table, sat a sword—a claymore, if Sanu had to guess—and a suit of armor big enough that both Sanu and Jab could've fit inside.

As the colossal hamster approached them, there was no doubt in Sanu's mind: this was Prince Ridgerd, the military man, the stories of whose exploits traveled farther than sailing ships.

According to the rumors floating out of traders' lips, Ridgerd had never lost a fight, and personally ensured his victory by leading his troops from the front, never wasting a second on traveling communication. Sanu told himself that couldn't possibly be true, since nobody could be that important and survive that long where the fighting was toughest. He definitely wanted to try his paw at picking up that giant sword though.

On his right, a trumpeter porcupine who seemed like a child compared to Ridgerd blew a horn the length of a walking stick. "Guests of Graganet Castle, you stand before King Ridgerd the First, son of the late beloved King Hedgry, recently crowned by Sapling Galdwin."

All the Sprouters with them except Lady Marjitay snapped their attention to a beaver behind Ridgerd, and Sanu recognized the Sapling's clothes. He couldn't remember every-thing about this religion, but he knew by the Sapling title that Galdwin must be important too.

Ridgerd narrowed his eyes at the chained mole rat. "Lady Marjitay? Why are you here in chains?" His voice carried the edge of battle.

"Treachery, of course," she replied. "Wait until you hear about my unfair treatment while we've been sailing."

"My liege, see the missive I have from Qawar." Sir Brouglas stepped forward. "It will explain."

Sanu noticed that Sir Brouglas didn't say ZelZaytun or the Sprouter name for it of "Olihort," using the island's name instead of the city's.

The beaver brought forward his message from Nasalid, and motioned for Sanu and Jandi to do the same.

Lady Marjitay grumbled as they did. "They chained me. That dog Nasalid sent me here to embarrass me and insult you."

The colossal hamster arched an eyebrow, and waved for attendants to grab the offered messages. "We'll give my men a moment to read this missive."

The Sapling, a graying beaver, rose from his smaller throne and lumbered forward. "I want to hear what the Protector of Olihort has to say first."

Ridgerd faced the Sapling and glowered. "I beseech you, O holy one, please accept my royal counsel in my chamber." The acid dripping from his voice made Sanu cringe.

"What's going on?" Jab whispered.

Sanu had no idea how to translate everything quickly for Jab, so he ignored him. He'd tell him later.

One attendant, a hamster a head shorter than Ridgerd, piped up. "My lord, Nasalid has taken control of Qawar, including the Holy City. He has stated that Sprouters can remain in the city and visit on pilgrimage, provided they don't bring weapons with them."

"He's taunting you, Ridgerd," Lady Marjitay spat. "He'll murder anyone who arrives."

Sanu's eyes widened and he looked to Jandi and Brouglas.

The beaver knight slapped his tail, stealing everyone's attention. "That is not true, my liege. I swore an oath to her, but I have disavowed myself because of what she did. She murdered a Sapling."

Jandi and the others in their group voiced agreement. Sanu pulled Jab close to him and stepped forward. "We saw it happen. She killed him with a crossbow."

Gasps rang out, and Ridgerd leaned closer.

"What did you just say to them?" Jab whispered.

"The truth," Sanu hissed back, debating if he should apologize to Jab for getting upset about *his* earlier outburst.

"You'd take the word of a child, an enemy, and a traitor over a noble?" The mole rat pointed at Sanu, Jandi, and Brouglas in turn. "The Sapling made a dirty deal with Nasalid. I was protecting the city. I'm sorry to say my love for Olihort was not enough to save it from the faithless Grovekeeper horde."

Sanu's jaw dropped.

Sir Brouglas placed a paw over his heart. "On my life, she does not speak true."

The beaver Sapling hobbled to Ridgerd's side. "Her word takes precedence over the knight's, legally. She is right that we cannot trust this delegation."

Ridgerd furrowed his brow. "None of this matters. Olihort is lost."

Sanu watched the royal hamster, unable to read what hid in his voice and expression. Was it guilt, grief, relief, confusion? He wished he could pry open his head and peer inside for some answers.

The king sighed and retreated to his throne. "My father's final order is now moot."

With a gasp, the Sapling wheeled on him. "Preposterous. It's more important now than ever."

Sir Brouglas stepped away from Lady Marjitay. "What was King Hedgry's final order?"

"To bolster the defenses at Olihort," Ridgerd said, running a wide paw through his hair. "He had a hunch Nasalid would assault the city."

"So take Olihort back," Lady Marjitay hissed.

The Sapling nodded ferociously. "Yes, King Ridgerd. You must reclaim the Holy City. Your grandfather and hers together led the glorious army to conquer the holy land, Ganan's own home, Blest be Him."

At the mention of Ganan the Gardener, all the Sprouters bowed their heads except Marjitay.

Sanu nudged his brother. "This is really bad. They're saying—"

The Sapling stomped his hindpaw and tail in unison. "King Ridgerd, if you wish to honor your father, you must reconquer Olihort."

"I don't have an army big or strong enough," the hamster king replied. "I won't wage war just to doom soldiers."

Some of the tension left Sanu's shoulders. Maybe it was true that real warriors knew when not to fight. "Maybe not so bad," Sanu whispered to Jab. "I think—"

The Sapling turned from the king and addressed the group. "I'll get approval from the Arborist, but I know he'll support me on this. I declare that anyone who enlists in King Ridgerd's army will be named a holy pilgrim. All their sins will be removed, and they will be guaranteed access to the Walled Garden after they die." He faced Ridgerd. "Even sins some would call unforgivable. You'd like that, wouldn't you, my king?" Where Ridgerd had previously spoken to him with acid in his voice, the Sapling had nothing but ice in his.

King Ridgerd rose from his throne and grabbed his sword. "It seems I have no choice. I fight for Olihort or I spend the afterlife in the Droughtlands." With voice lowered and sword raised, he added, "To war."

5

JAB

- Divine Poetics.

The next few days felt like a blur. Not knowing the language, Jab felt tethered to Sanu, though he began picking up phrases. Yagub and Brouglas made sure nobody bothered them, and they prayed at the designated times with Jandi in what felt like a prison sentence. They got meals, and nobody forced them to eat anything with olives, but it felt like they were under observation. Some of Ridgerd's castle attendants watched them like one watches flies buzz around a dead bird, and others stared at them like they were exhibits in a museum.

Jandi never removed his armor, even in his sleep. The few words Jab could get out of him were all the same. "Don't trust these snakes. Don't bother learning their language." Jab nodded each time Jandi said that, but he did enjoy learning the language.

As big as Castle Graganet felt, the quarters grew cramped. Thanks to Sir Brouglas's testimony, they were allowed to join the ship bound for Qawar, so they could serve as translators and intermediaries between Ridgerd and Nasalid. Jab didn't need any translation help to decipher what was happening across the castle as each day passed.

Soldiers poured in, as did ships.

The Sapling's promise must have spread far and fast.

For two weeks, Jab's prayers were all he had to mark the time. His lessons in Frenglese took place beside Brouglas's lessons in Qawari. The jovial beaver was much preferred over that crotchety Sapling. Even though Jab knew Sanu probably left out some details from the first meeting, he sensed the pressure the Sapling had placed on Ridgerd. Getting all sins forgiven was a powerful motivator for anyone, yet it seemed to Sanu like the Sapling had tried to make it personal.

When it was time for the ships to depart, Jab didn't know much beyond the fact that they were taking the faster route around Coppergrass Isle instead of the coastal route they'd used coming here. He had no clue what or where Coppergrass was, but at least he'd be home sooner. Jab just wished his homecoming wasn't in the vanguard of a war he was supposed to prevent.

Sanu, Brouglas, and Yagub were equally dejected, but Jandi seemed more upset that they'd wasted everyone's time than about the impending fight.

"Nasalid might as well have said, 'come and get me, pellet-eaters,'" Jandi said as they boarded the ship.

"I don't think Ridgerd would've been as reluctant to wage war if he had," Yagub retorted. "You saw how conflicted he was."

Seagulls cried overhead, and Jab wondered if they were happy about the departing sailors, cheering them on. Jab counted the ships and gave up once he realized there were over one hundred. "How many soldiers are gathered here?"

Brouglas hefted a crate onto the deck. "If full, all of them, thousands of tens."

"He means tens of thousands," Sanu said, almost with excitement.

How could anyone be excited about a massive force ready to invade their home? It seemed like Dad's scimitar was the only thing about Sanu that Jab recognized anymore. He'd changed so much in his time with the Sprouters, and all Jab had were his regrets and nightmares.

The ship felt crowded, especially since room was made for Lady Marjitay, though not in shackles. Jab wondered how she'd connived her way into new clothes and a seat of power, and he wondered if she meant to be part of a triumphant return to ZelZaytun, renaming it Olihort, and re-enacting the slaughter of Jab's grandparents' time.

Sailing on the king's ship should have been exhilarating, but for Jab, this was just a royal reminder of his failure. The logical part of his brain knew that he couldn't have done anything to change the course of events—he wasn't even trusted with a copy of Nasalid's message, despite that same Liberator calling Jab the "savior of Rattin." But the emotional part of Jab knew that if he had truly followed the All-Planter's plan, none of this would be happening.

The Divine Poetics said that all it took to convert a non-believer was to act in honest kindness toward them, and if that didn't work, to increase the kindness. Maybe Jab hadn't been kind enough. As the sailing cog left the harbor, he remembered his unkind thoughts about Lady Marjitay. Maybe the All-Planter was punishing him.

Jab gazed over the deck, and Jandi came to his side. The older squirrel was an image of what Dad might have looked like in a few years.

Jab's spirits lifted, hoping Jandi would have some kind words of understanding to share.

"Your crossbow," Jandi said, not making eye contact, "did they ever give it back to you?"

"What?" Jab asked.

Jandi scoffed. "Do you have barnacles in your ears already? You got a crossbow for joining the Liberator's scout corps, didn't you?"

Jab nodded, remembering the weapon, and how he'd fired it at Sanu during the siege, not knowing who he was.

"Well, where is it? The Frenglese took it from you, didn't they?"

"I never unpacked it from my belongings," Jab said. "I didn't really like carrying it around."

Jandi tutted and pushed himself off the rail. "I bet the Goose herself got someone to loot through your things and take it. Someone would've taken your brother's weapon if the beaver knight hadn't convinced everyone that it was a training blade. Mark my words, they'll throw us overboard when they get a chance. You, me, your brother, the Qawari Sprouter, and the beaver knight."

Jab arched an eyebrow. "After sailing and spending so much time in the castle together, you never learned Yagub and Brouglas's names?"

"They're our enemies, boy. I don't learn the names of the bugs I step on or the trees I cut down. You shouldn't either."

Behind them, Sanu and Brouglas sparred, scimitar against falchion, with sailors and soldiers cheering them on.

"They're savages," Jandi continued. "Eating olives. They might as well spit on the All-Planter. It's disgusting."

Staring up at the darkening clouds, Jab shook his head. His gaze fell back on the water, and he noticed one of the ships in the flotilla—the one he thought had the most soldiers—start veering off-course.

"Should that ship be going that way?" Jab asked.

"It's full of barbarians who will ruin our home," Jandi replied. "It can turn around or go to the bottom of the ocean for all I care."

6

SANU

I have sent along with Lady Marjitay one of her former knights. He can attest to her murder of ZelZaytun's Sapling, as can my sergeant who is with him and the young brothers. With these three copies of my message, my prayer is that you will accept the truth of my words.

- Excerpt from Nasalid the Liberator's message to the Frenglese kings.

Darkening clouds promised rain. Sanu readied his scimitar to parry Sir Brouglas's half-speed onslaught.

"Watch your hindpaw position," Yagub called from the side.

Sir Brouglas pivoted, slapping Sanu's knee with his tail and knocking him off balance. The sailing cog bobbed, sharper than it had since they'd departed. The waves must be getting choppy. Either way, Sanu dropped to a knee.

"Told you," Yagub said.

Sanu brushed it off and lunged for the knight.

Over by the railing Jab and Jandi talked, watching the swirling ocean. Sanu assumed Jandi was still on his "they're going to kill us" tear, which was why he was wearing his full set of armor.

Sanu paused—one of the transport cogs was going off-course.

Brouglas smacked Sanu with the blunt side of his falchion. "Stay focused, lad."

"Loser has latrine duty!" a soldier called.

Sanu smirked. "Is 'latrine duty' a nickname for Lady Marjitay?"

A roar of guffaws came, but Brouglas's expression hardened.

He sheathed his falchion. "Don't say such things about rodents. I thought you were more noble than that. That's not something a real warrior would do. We honor and protect others, even with our words."

Sanu took a step back. An adult hadn't been visibly disappointed in him since his parents were alive. He hoped Jab didn't hear over the rain or couldn't understand the Frenglese words.

As a crack of thunder punctured the sky, Sanu realized Brouglas wasn't the only one in the gathered crowd who hadn't joined in the laughter. Rain smacked the deck, and most of the soldiers dispersed. Heavy rivulets slithered off Brouglas's whiskers, and Yagub stared at his hindpaws.

Sanu blinked hard. "I-I'm sorry," he stammered.

While the crowd thinned, footsteps approached. An umbrella with a stitched-on goose pattern came forward, held aloft by the scowling Lady Marjitay.

"Say that again," she hissed.

Sir Brouglas came between them. "My lady, he's just a lad. Boys say silly things. Please don't—"

She backpawed Brouglas across the face. "Shut up." She turned to the attendant to her left. "Send this boy to the same cage I was in. I'm sure it's around here somewhere."

"What?" Sanu shouted. "You're a murderer! You can't lock me up."

As the cog struggled over a wave, the ship's deck came up at a sharp angle.

The storm increased in intensity, attacking the ship from above and below. He needed to get below deck, but not into a cage. She belonged in one.

"Take his weapon too," the mole rat added. "Whoever does will get a spot on my honor guard when we retake Olihort."

Sanu's eyes widened, and a few soldiers exchanged glances, then turned to face Sanu, who struggled to keep balance in the choppy waters.

The ship rocked hard right, and Sanu lost his footing, as did half the soldiers and Lady Marjitay. They tilted so steeply that Sanu managed a good look at his brother, where he clutched the railing for dear life, too far away for Sanu to pull him to safety.

Jab's grip failed and Sanu forgot to breathe. Not too long ago, he thought he'd watched Jab consumed by fire. As Jab and Jandi screamed for help, Sanu was helpless to see raging water do what fire could not. In the middle of a storm and in the middle of the ocean, Jab fell over the railing.

"Jab!" Sanu shouted, scrambling to stand, but slipping on the rain-slick deck. "I'm coming! Jab!"

Jandi lunged over the railing, clutching Jab's wrist, groaning against the pounding rain. But it wasn't enough. Jandi fell overboard.

Sanu rose on shaky legs, but another sharp wave dropped him to his behind.

Stomping against the tipping ship, Sir Brouglas, strong enough to run up a wet surface and tear off his armor at the same time, ran to the railing and dove overboard.

Sanu had been too weak and too slow to save Jab, but he had to help Brouglas. Fighting the rain and unsteady ship, he rose to his hindpaws, pushing himself up with his tail. No storm would take Jab away from him.

The ship righted, and heavy arms wrapped around Sanu. A sailor had snatched him.

"Put me down," Sanu shouted, legs dangling midair. "Somebody help them!"

Sopping wet, Lady Marjitay stood in front of him. "No. We all need to get below deck. You, in particular. Keep talking and you'll join them."

7

JAB

Heat bore down on Jab's body, and his fur stank like salty fish. A hard force pushed on his chest, and he wondered if this was how it felt to die, or if it was already Pruning Day and he'd have to account for his life in front of the All-Planter. He remembered waves tossing him about.

A *whoom whoomp whoomp* thudded nearby, muffled by something grainy. Sand in his ears? Perhaps he'd sunk to the ocean's bottom, and the sun reached farther than anyone thought. It was a nice idea.

Whoom whoomp

Jab's eyes opened and a *splurt* of water jetted from his mouth.

The harsh sun assaulted his eyes, and Jab coughed up more water.

"You with me?"

Blinking hard, Jab sat bolt upright. It was Sir Brouglas. They were on a beach, sopping wet, with no ships visible anywhere.

"What happened? Where are we?" Jab's voice grated on his own ears like salt had lodged in his throat.

The beaver plopped on the sand beside him, catching his breath. "You fell over in the storm. The grouchy one also."

The grouchy one? "Jandi?"

Brouglas nodded. "Sorry. I could not save both you. His armor sank him. I took off mine before swimming."

Jab's stomach twisted, but not from the ocean water. "He wore that around because he thought someone was going to attack him."

"I wish it was not that way. The Honky Goose set her claws into the Sapling, and no one can say no to them." The beaver knight stood, extending a paw.

Jab accepted and stood, feeling light-headed. He didn't have his crossbow anymore. First, he'd lost Mom's prayer rock, and now he'd lost Nasalid's weapon. Nothing was safe with him. Jab met Brouglas's eyes. "Thank you for saving me."

"Squirrels climb. Beavers swim. Such is the way of things." He offered a weak smile.

"Do you know where we are?" Jab turned around and saw thin trees poking over the horizon where grass and sand commingled. "This isn't Qawar."

"No, lad," Brouglas said. "And we're not in Freng." He scratched the back of his head. "I don't know how to say the name in your language, but look at the shore. We're on the west side of this island, closer to the Freng islands. If we want to get to Qawar, we need to get on the east side."

Jab sighed. "So we're stuck here? Are there rodents here friendly to Nasalid who could take us to Qawar?" A twinge of guilt pulled in Jab's heart. He hadn't given a single thought to his brother in his few minutes of consciousness, and his first real concern was for a man who sent him away.

"Coppergrass," Brouglas said. "Coppergrass Isle."

"Excuse me?" Jab wondered if that was another way to say "sand."

"That's the name of this place in your language. Lots of metal in the soil. It makes the grass look like copper."

He'd seen this island on maps, but he'd thought it was supposed to be lined with mountains all around it, like the island was some grand bowl. He didn't love the idea of maps he'd spent time studying being wrong.

"Brouglas, where is Sanu?"

"He wanted to save you, lad, but Lady Marjitay *grapped* him."

Jab wondered how to politely correct him. "Sanu was grabbed? Like captured?"

"He insulted Marjitay." Brouglas's tone soured. "I was not happy with his words."

Jab knew he shouldn't be proud of his brother for insulting someone, but he was a little bit because it was Lady Marjitay. And then his old guilt returned; the All-Planter demanded equal love to all rodents. Jab needed to work on that. Remembering Lady Marjitay's affinity for crossbows, Jab crunched some sand between his toes. "Is she going to kill Sanu?"

Brouglas slammed his tail into the sand. "Ridgerd would never let her." He muttered in Frenglese, and all Jab caught were the words for "no," "never," and "not him." The beaver breathed deep and switched languages. "Ridgerd was at the Battle of Phranktonbourg. I was too. He is a noble hamster, lad."

Jab wondered if that was a city in Freng somewhere, but didn't want to press. He'd touched a nerve and a memory that didn't need to come to the surface now. "I'm glad to hear that. But where should we go now?"

Sir Brouglas pointed into the distance, beyond the tiny trees that could've been thin bushes. "We get higher, then we maybe see the town, I think."

Jab followed him, sinking more into the sand with each step as the coarse grains softened. Before, he measured where he was by how far he was from home, but he didn't know in which direction anything was, not Qawar, not Sanu, and not peace. Ridgerd would descend on Qawar like a storm and there was nothing he could do to stop it. Jab's throat tightened as they worked their way up the beach, drying his bushy tail in the sun.

"Never been here," Brouglas said. "Good fruits, I know that."

Anything but citrus would be wonderful. The aroma of apple and pear wafted into Jab's mental nose. "What kinds?"

"Oranges and lemons," the beaver said with a smile. "When I first came to Qawar, I ate them on the ship. Good sailing food."

The last grains of sand disappeared, and Jab noticed the metallic brown tint in the grass. It crunched the same way as the grass back home. The same seagulls circled around the sky and patrolled the beach too. Maybe he wasn't so far from home. But as they neared the trees, he realized that some were actually his size. Knowing that a Gnaverwood was also a tree, calling this thing anything other than a bush felt ridiculous.

The hill sloped up further and Jab strained his neck upon seeing the tips of a rooftop peeking over the hill's crest. He knew it was a roof because it had the dome shape like those back in ZelZaytun and Rattin, but he spied the shape of Ganan's Rake atop it. A small pit rose in Jab's stomach. He'd thought Grovekeepers would've lived here, not Sprouters.

"I thought I knew what this place would be like. I looked at maps of the Great Sea once," Jab said.

Brouglas arched an eyebrow. "All?"

"Well, just the area around Qawar, I suppose." Jab hoped he didn't sound stupid. "The town name I remember seeing was ZelNuhas, and there was a city named Huzn."

Brouglas shook his head, starting up the hill. "Those are Qawar names. They speak Frenglese here. This may be Rado Town."

As they reached the top of the hill, more domed mudbrick buildings with Ganan's Rakes appeared, bleached white by the sun. Faint noise and chatter nearby told him this was a smaller town, maybe even a village.

Between the two nearest buildings, a burly rodent faced Brouglas and Jab, a mole rat. He wielded a crossbow, pointed between the two of them.

He spoke in something garbled that almost felt familiar, but Brouglas didn't seem to quite understand either. Jab and Brouglas raised their paws in the air and inched backward. The mole rat cranked his crossbow and said something else they couldn't understand.

But Jab didn't need a translator to know they had trespassed.

8

SANU

*- General Ironseed's reprimand
to a failed sergeant.*

Sanu rattled his cage, imagining Lady Marjitay snarling as she pulled the trigger on a crossbow and killed him, maybe the same one she'd used on the porcupine Sapling during the ZelZaytun siege. To think he once believed he'd die as a great legendary warrior. He'd die in a windowless room without seeing his homeland or brother again.

Sanu was glad Jab wouldn't see him like this. He hoped the ship that got blown off-course picked up Jab, Brouglas, and Jandi, although Jandi would've found a reason to complain if they had. The possibility of his brother being alive on another ship brought a small comfort.

Above him, the cabin door opened, letting light pour in, showing the storm had stopped. Heavy pawsteps thudded against the creaky wood stairs.

Sanu lacked the courage to keep his eyes open.

The steps didn't patter like a noble's slipper, but carried the heavy cadence of someone big. Huge, even. And there were two sets, one much heavier than the other.

Sanu opened his eyes—King Ridgerd and Yagub stood before him.

The hamster could barely stand up straight in the cramped space. "Yagub tells me you speak Frenglese well. Is this so?"

"Y-yes," Sanu replied. "I learned it from him and the current Sapling of ZelZaytun."

Memories of Cladh warmed his heart, but he was too busy getting ready to die to have time to think about her right now.

Ridgerd nodded and turned to Yagub. "I'd like you to stay, in case there are translation issues."

"Of course, my lord." Yagub almost sounded like a different rodent without Brouglas around.

Sanu's heart tightened. *Brouglas wasn't around.*

That other ship would've come back to the main fleet by now. The storm had calmed down. Brouglas would have demanded a rowboat to return to the king's ship if they had picked them up, so he'd be here if he'd come back. That meant Jab and Jandi weren't back either.

Ridgerd pulled a stool in front of Sanu's cage and sat down, though even when seated, he was still too tall for Sanu to look him in the eye without craning his neck.

"I wasn't on deck when the incident happened," Ridgerd said. "I need you to repeat your words about Lady Marjitay."

Yagub's whiskers drooped. "I'm sure he feels awful about it, sire, I—"

The king held up a paw, keeping his eye on Sanu. "Speak, boy."

Sanu's throat dried, bringing back memories of the desert back home. "It was an unkind joke, good king. It went too far."

"I do like hearing 'good king,'" the hamster said, tapping his crown, "but repeat your words."

Sanu closed his eyes and counted to five in his head. "While sparring with Sir Brouglas, a sailor taunted me, saying that whoever lost our match would have latrine duty. I, um, I asked if 'latrine duty' was a nickname for Lady Marjitay."

Sanu stared at his hindpaws, ready for the proclamation of death.

"Ha!" Ridgerd's laugh came so strongly that Sanu nearly jumped out of his fur. "Did you happen to see her face when you said that?" King Ridgerd's body shook, fighting to contain the laughter.

Sanu wasn't sure if this meant he was safe or if the king was insane. "N-no. If I'd known she was there, I wouldn't have said anything."

Yagub sidled against the cage. "I assure you, sire, when we showed him the kindness of Sprouters back in the Holy City, we only taught him manners and proper speech."

Sanu wondered why Yagub was on edge, but realization hit like lightning. Yagub was Qawari like Sanu, even though they followed different religions. Brouglas was the only knight aboard who could vouch for and protect Yagub, and that support system had jumped overboard.

"Latrine duty." Ridgerd wiped a tear from the corner of his eye and sighed. "I'm laughing, but don't say things like that about rodents. Between the three of us, you practically gave her a compliment."

Sanu gulped. "King Ridgerd, what'll happen to me?"

The hamster rose from his stool, careful not to bonk his head against the rafters and pointed at his crown. "You've received a stern warning from the king. You will apologize, swearing to use kinder words in public."

Yagub sighed and his shoulders relaxed. "He won't be executed then?" His gaze turned to Sanu. "I tried to talk her out of it."

"And that was your mistake," Ridgerd replied. "Nobles can't take a joke. It's one of their many flaws. I should know. Yagub, after you left, she wanted your hide as well."

Yagub's tail stiffened.

"No!" Sanu cried. "He's a good squirrel, he—"

Ridgerd held up a paw. "You're both too useful to be thrown overboard. You both know Qawar as a land and a language. I'll need that, and so will my lieutenants. Nobody aboard likes the Honking Goose, but she's promised land and titles to whoever helps her. So watch your words." He made a key turning motion with his fingers, and Yagub pawed him a key. "If you ever have anything so vile to say about the Honking Goose of Olihort," the king stooped down and unlocked Sanu's cage, "come find me and we'll laugh about it together. From now on, you both will be visiting me and teaching me about Qawar."

He offered a paw and Sanu accepted, stepping out of the cage. Both of Sanu's paws could've fit in one of Ridgerd's.

"Remember, use kind words in public, young squirrel. We have a few more days' sailing to get to Qawar, and I can't have you locked up again. Come on. We'll get you dry clothes."

The king started up the stairs, and Sanu stared at his paws.

Now he was lost at sea, a world apart from the brother he'd been too slow to save. A pitter-patter above him suggested the rain wasn't done either.

9

JAB

The mole rat advanced, and Jab and Brouglas kept razor-straight and still. Jab hadn't survived a concussion, an attack by a madrodent, and falling into the Great Sea, just to die at a stranger's paws on this island he never wanted to visit. He'd dreamed of a future in Qawar, in the shade of ZelZaytun's holy Gnaverwood tree.

Maybe if Brouglas still had his armor, they'd stand a chance.

The mole rat mumbled something, and Jab could've sworn he heard the Qawari word for "who" and the Frenglese word for "you."

Brouglas, though stiff, spoke in Frenglese, using simple words that Jab could follow. "We are travelers. We are lost."

Heart racing, Jab decided to try his luck in Qawari. "We are travelers. We are lost."

"Bandits," the mole rat hissed.

That word Jab understood clearly.

"We are not bandits," Jab said. "We are on a journey. We don't know where we are."

The mole rat lowered his crossbow a fraction. He shouted something unintelligible.

A hamster poked a head around the side of a house and tiptoed forward. Since the last hamster Jab had seen was King Ridgerd, this one seemed like a dwarf hamster, but after thinking about it for a second, he understood this hamster was a standard adult woman. She waved a paw to Brouglas and then to Jab, bowing slightly.

"I heard Qawari," she said to Jab. Turning her gaze to Brouglas, she switched languages. "And I heard Frenglese. My parents were copper traders, so I speak both." Her cadence and word choice made it easier for Jab to understand her. She muttered something to the mole rat, and he lowered his crossbow all the way.

Jab arched an eyebrow. "That language you spoke to him, it sounded like Frenglese and Qawari, mashed together."

"Aye," Brouglas added. "I caught some of it."

The hamster smiled. "I should think so. The rodents of Coppergrass Isle have roots from all over the Great Sea, mostly from the Frenglese archipelago and Qawar. Most of us in Rado Town are Sprouters, but there are Grovekeepers and

Mulchers all around too, especially in Newhouse City a little way south. My friend told me there was a group of Llygodeners here but I've never met them. Anyway, living here together for so long, the languages joined together."

"Then that's why we understood some words." Brouglas slapped his tail against the dirt. "Your friend said something about bandits. I assure you; we are travelers."

The hamster folded her arms over her chest. "Travelers or shipwrecked sailors? There is a difference." Her dress was a bit cleaner than the mole rat's clothes. It seemed like it was made with a nicer fabric, but Jab didn't have a great eye for that.

Jab's cheeks flushed. They weren't shipwrecked, not really. He'd fallen overboard and Brouglas sacrificed himself to save him.

Brouglas didn't respond either.

The hamster stepped forward and the mole rat gripped his crossbow again. "Unless you're lying to me and you are with the bandits. Or maybe you're smugglers? Thieves?"

Brouglas shook his head. "My sword and armor are back on our boat, so I can't prove it, but I am a knight in service of King Ridgerd."

Staring at his hindpaws, Jab added, "I fell overboard on our ship. He saved me and we washed ashore here."

"I see. Well, in that case, I'm glad you survived, and welcome to Rado Town, the quiet farm community which feeds the eastern side of Coppergrass," the hamster said. "My name is Gizlee, and you already met Yumruk." She indicated her mole rat friend. "Now, I hate to be a bad host, but he wasn't kidding about the bandits. I don't have anywhere for you to stay."

"Where would bandits come from on such a small island?" Jab asked.

Yumruk eyed Gizlee, and she waved him off. "I have no problem telling them. They don't stink like the bandits. Besides," she turned her head toward Brouglas. "I don't know of any beavers who joined Nasalid's army, do you?"

Jab's eyes nearly bulged from his head. "N-Nasalid? The Liberator?" She was right though. In his time walking through Nasalid's camps, he'd seen other squirrels, gerbils, jerboas, and Nasalid as the sole jird, but no beavers. He wasn't sure any even lived in Qawar except for the colonists from Freng, like Brouglas.

"You've heard of him?" Gizlee asked. "These bandits have too. They deserted his army."

"Deserted?" Brouglas asked.

"You can talk to them about it," Gizlee said. "They're eating our town's food in the tavern."

Heart pounding, Jab didn't want to ask who in their right minds would desert the Liberator. He was noble, he treated everyone kindly, and—

That's when it hit Jab. Nasalid *was* noble and kind, even to the defeated enemy. Nasalid had forbidden looting and insisted all prisoners be treated as if they were regular soldiers, receiving the same rations and medical attention as everyone else. Jab remembered the grumbles well. It led a few awful rodents to betray him. Apparently, it led others here.

Jab clenched his fist. "We'll send those bandits on a boat going straight to their homes, you'll see."

Brouglas hit Jab's shoulder with an open paw, right on the line between loving, encouraging, and sheer pain. "I'd prefer to do it with a sword, but the boy speaks true. We'll get those bandits out of your fur. Show us the way."

Gizlee arched an eyebrow, and motioned for Yumruk to follow her. Rado Town reminded Jab of Rattin, his hometown. The place was more of a road intersection that had grown slowly than a planned town. Rows of small shops lined the street, with a few rows of homes behind or above them.

The road bisecting the town stretched across the horizon to the east and west, and Jab searched again for a Gnaverwood tree, but none were in sight. Why anyone would live here was beyond him. As they walked by the buildings, he appreciated the familiar architecture, but his heart sank after seeing all the boarded-up homes.

There was even a Grovekeeper prayer hall sitting beside a Gananshed—both religions' holy buildings. That brightened his spirits, not in the hopes that the rodents here would become Grovekeepers, but that the two religions could get along side by side, unlike how things had been back home before Nasalid's rise to power.

Yet in these streets, not a single rodent came out to greet them. Instead, Jab caught glimpses of rodents whispering and watching them from behind closed doors and through cracks in the boarded-up windows.

"We used to have soldiers protecting these farms and shops," Gizlee said with a heavy voice. "But there was a ... change in power recently, and the new leader of Rado Town is ... not quite effective. But he is better than the island's new ruler."

Yumruk scoffed, polishing his crossbow as they walked.

Gizlee eyed Brouglas. "You said you served King Ridgerd. You'll have to excuse me, but how long has he had the throne? A ... dear friend of mine was niece to King Hedgry. She was killed by the baroness. King Ridgerd should know."

"That's a funny way to say you knew the Bachelorette Queen," Brouglas said. "I'm sorry for your loss. Ridgerd has been king for a month." Brouglas bowed in front of the Gananshed as they passed, never taking his eyes off the rake symbol atop it. "King Hedgry died suddenly. It was quite the shock."

"My condolences. So the war prince Ridgerd has taken the throne." Gizlee rubbed her chin. "I heard he's been criticized for never taking a wife. My friend was insulted because she never had or wanted a husband." Gizlee cast an eye at Jab. "I have been too, but only by my family and the seedlings."

Jab watched her, trying to figure out what was going on in her mind, but remembered Dad's words about how the only language men could never learn was a woman's thoughts. He also remembered how Mom would groan after he said that.

As they neared the inn at the end of the village, Jab's heart pulsed. These rodents were once in

Nasalid's army, and they might have been in it at the same time as Jab. There was a chance they'd recognize him and kill him for fun.

Inhaling deep, Jab knew there was another possibility. He could convince them to abandon their ways and rejoin Nasalid to defend it against the upcoming attack.

Jab had to try to stop these bandits with Brouglas. It's what Sanu would do. Above, the clouds darkened and raindrops descended on the rooftops like drums.

War drums.

10

SANU

You should know that when ZelZaytun capitulated to my forces, there was a call to execute or ransom the prisoners. Instead I took the suggestion of one of the boys I have sent to you, Jab of Rattin, to cleanse the city with rosewater instead of Sprouter blood. I declare the slaughter of ZelZaytun's citizens two generations ago forgiven, yet painfully remembered. Our feud for this city may end.

- Excerpt from Nasalid the Liberator's message to the Frenglese kings.

Sanu, walking beside Yagub, followed King Ridgerd up the rickety ship steps, and a growing commotion above deck intensified. The mighty hamster swung open the cabin door to a torrent of rain, and Sanu wondered who else would fall overboard this time. Sailors scurried about to secure the sails, their stomping the only thing louder than the rain.

"What is all this shouting?" King Ridgerd demanded.

"A ship got separated from the fleet and still hasn't returned!" a sailor wailed, holding his hat tight against the wind.

Sanu's heart raced and he dared to inch closer to the king. Maybe this would mean Ridgerd would call off the invasion. Maybe the All-Planter had destroyed one ship to save Qawar from a disastrous war. It wasn't enough of a consolation to ease his brother's disappearance though.

"Where?" the hamster king roared. "Why wasn't I informed earlier?"

The group of sailors running around the ship grabbing supplies stopped in their tracks. Only the rain carried on in defiance of the king.

"T-toward Coppergrass Isle, my liege. Blown off-course."

The king turned toward the ship's pilot, a porcupine desperately grasping the steering rudder.

"Then turn us toward Coppergrass! We won't abandon our brothers." King Ridgerd swiveled left and right. "Where's the first mate? Signal the other ships." A deckpaw had slipped into the railing, and Ridgerd rushed to help him stand.

Sanu wiped the rainwater from his face. He both admired and despised the king in that moment. He wished he would've somehow heeded Sanu's hope of calling off the invasion. Searching Yagub's eyes, Sanu noticed the respect in them. Something about the king inspired confidence and trust, and it wasn't the crown.

Ridgerd rushed to the pulley for the main sail and helped a team of sailors raise it. "Come on," the king howled, "let's find our brothers! No rodent left behind!"

Wavering in the strengthening rain, the ship's pilot saluted the king. Sailors on this ship and the others in the flotilla secured the triangular sails. The synchronization was impressive, even though it meant these rodents would still descend on Qawar.

"Belay that order!"

Sanu recognized that voice. It was Sapling Galdwin who had pressured Ridgerd into waging the war. Sanu shivered. He'd forgotten that foul beaver—a cruel reminder of Brouglas— was aboard.

"We will continue to the Holy City," Galdwin insisted. "It was the All-Planter's will that they be lost at sea. We cannot wait another moment."

With one sailor clutching her umbrella, Lady Marjitay resurfaced. "No one is keeping me from my throne."

Eyes shifted toward Ridgerd, and Sanu's insides felt like a hyena was on the loose. This was even worse.

The king inhaled more air than Sanu would've guessed possible, probably along with some rain water. The hamster turned away from the Sapling and the lady, facing the crowd of sailors. "A holy test of faith from our holy guide!" He glared at the Sapling over his shoulder for a flash before turning back to the soldiers and sailors. "In his wisdom, the Sapling is testing us. He is seeing if we remember the words of Ganan the Gardener, Blest be Him."

"Blest be Him," the sailors chorused.

"Our Lord taught us that there is no greater sacrifice than to help a doomed friend. We must save our brothers on that ship." With an exhale, he slowly turned to face the Sapling. "Thank you, Galdwin. You surely have the All-Planter's wisdom to test us in the rain like this. None of us saw it coming."

Sanu stepped closer to Ridgerd, getting protection from both the downpour and the Honking Goose.

Lady Marjitay snarled and approached Ridgerd, nearly stepping on Sanu. "You tell them to keep going. We're getting my throne one way or another."

"We can't take Olihort back without a full army," Ridgerd said. "You can be patient."

"Patient?" Her voice blended into the rain. "I know why you're so hesitant to go there and why you were eager to leave home."

The king's expression turned to a dark scowl. "Watch your tongue. I am still a king."

"Without a queen. Why is that, Ridgerd?" Her voice turned Sanu's stomach. There was something in her tone he couldn't understand because she asked the question, even though it sounded like she knew the answer. Dad had told Sanu once that women spoke two languages at once half the time, and it was impossible to translate. He wasn't sure if that was the whole saying. Jab would remember and probably say that Dad didn't have the most enlightened views about women, since men could speak with hidden meanings too. Sanu had learned that the hard way with the nobles back in ZelZaytun.

Yagub placed a paw on Sanu's shoulder and pulled gently, but Sanu didn't budge. He needed to hear Ridgerd's response.

The hamster stooped to get in her ear, but he didn't lower his voice. "I've been busy fighting for my father, and now I'm fighting for Ganan Himself, Blest be Him. We'll leave it there, *murderer*."

The mole rat folded her arms and stuck her nose in the air. "Whatever you need to tell yourself. I'll need a husband after we take Olihort back."

"There's not enough gold in the Walled Garden for that," Ridgerd scoffed. "Now get out of my way. These two are helping me and we need to get the rowboats ready to land on Coppergrass. Put on some hiking gear. The island is mostly hills, I hear."

The first mate, a beaver whose fur had grayed more from sea salt than age, bounded over. "The flotilla is signaled, sir."

"Good," the king said. "Take these two squirrels to my quarters and introduce them to Seedling Nett. Have everyone else get ready for landing."

"I know where to go," Yagub said, and he ushered Sanu to follow him, crossing the slippery deck. The relentless sheets of rain threatened Sanu's balance, making him worry about Jab even more. He just had to be alive.

They trudged across the deck toward the captain's cabin, a suite of rooms designated for the king, the Sapling, and Lady Marjitay. A teenage porcupine stood at the one unmarked door. She wore clothes similar to the hamster of his dreams back in ZelZaytun, the clothes of a holy Sprouter, a seedling. It made him miss Cladh even more.

Yagub took a hesitant step forward. "Hello, Madam Seedling. We were sent to you by King Ridgerd."

The porcupine waved her paw dismissively, and Sanu noticed how her clothes were modified for her quills. "Yes, I know, I've been waiting here *forever* for you." Her tone sounded more playful than annoyed, and her accent reminded him of Brouglas's.

"Um, we're sorry to have k-kept you," Yagub stuttered.

Sanu arched an eyebrow at the other squirrel. "We were speaking with the king and then Marjitay slowed him down by being obnoxious."

The porcupine chuckled. "I've heard about your name for her. I'd suggest using her 'Lady' title whenever you can."

Sanu had some less than kind remarks surface in his mind, but he shoved them down. "But the king didn't tell us why we needed to see you."

"Did he say my name at least?" she asked with a smile. "I'm Nett. I'm stuck ferrying messages between the Sapling and King Ridgerd, since they don't like each other much. We have a prayer space below this floor. It's not a nice Gananshed, but it'll do."

"Nett," Yagub repeated under his breath. "I-I'm Yagub, and this is Sanu."

"I know both of you," Nett replied, turning around and opening the unmarked door she'd been concealing with her quills. It led down a staircase to another part of the ship Sanu hadn't seen yet. It wasn't much different from the other rooms in size or shape, but it bore the same decorations of Ganan's Rake that adorned Nett's clothes. A simple gold table protruded from the wall, displaying some gold trinkets.

"Oh," Sanu said, realizing where they were. "I'm a Grovekeeper."

"I kno-o-ow," Nett replied in a gentle sing-song. "We aren't here to pray to Ganan, Blest be Him, but to talk. Yagub, could you pull up some chairs, please?"

The ship rocked with a wave, and Yagub stumbled over his tail as he turned. Sanu hoped whatever they had for chairs in this space weren't rake-shaped.

Yagub came over with three stools and set them on the floor.

Nett sat between Sanu and Yagub, facing them both. "I'm sorry if they are a bit uncomfortable; they weren't designed for squirrels. Not too many of you in Freng," she added with a chuckle.

"I'm fine," Sanu said. "But what are we doing here?"

"The King wanted you two to talk to me."

"But why?" Sanu pressed.

Yagub shoved Sanu's tail with his own, something Jab would do when they'd have secret fights in front of their parents.

Nett offered a gentle smile. "You watched your brother go overboard." She turned to Yagub. "And you lost your knight. Both of you must be devastated. King Ridgerd wanted you to talk through the pain with me. He and I speak often about his difficulties and worries."

Sanu scoffed. "What could possibly be difficult or worrisome for a king?"

"Sanu!" Yagub chided.

Nett's smile retreated into her face. "He has many worries. I am honor and oath bound to keep the specifics of our conversations private, but I can tell you that he fears going to the Droughtlands after he dies. He fears the All-Planter would never let him into the Walled Garden. The Sapling pressures him, as does the Arborist in Gananshire. His mother's skill at intrigue mostly kept them at bay when he was a prince, but there are more eyes on him now. Everyone tells him the only way to make up for his faults is to fight."

That didn't sound like keeping the specifics private to Sanu, but he wondered if there were other layers she wasn't explaining. "What faults does he have?" Sanu asked. *Besides his willingness to attack my home, that is.*

"Not everyone approves of Ridgerd, even though some things are outside his control," Nett replied. "But we're not here to discuss him. The two of you need to process your grief."

"I'm not grieving." Sanu folded his arms over his chest. "I'm worried about my *still alive* brother."

Yagub rubbed the sides of his head. "This might take a while."

JAB

- Raticenna's collected sermons

By the time Jab and Sir Brouglas reached the tavern door, the rain fell hard enough that entering a bandit's den was a relief. The ceiling rose high enough for an upper level and a chandelier hanging down from it. Long tapestries hung from the upper level balcony down to the match the chandelier's level. The drab fabrics rippled with the door opening, jostling the stylized image of Coppergrass isle decorating them.

When they entered and found a gang of armored squirrels, Jab regretted examining the interior first. His mouth dropped at the scowling snouts on these Qawari rodents, who wore leather armor with Grovekeeper symbols etched into them, slurping up fermented berry juice like common criminals. Some part of him was glad they weren't part of Nasalid's liberating army; scoundrels like these didn't deserve to experience the glory of a liberated ZelZaytun.

The six bandits slammed down their mugs. Swirling berry-stained froth splashed over their paws.

"Steady, friend," Brouglas whispered to Jab. "I will talk. Translate please if I need help."

"No," Jab said, stepping in front of him. "Hey!"

The six soldiers shoved their chairs backward, the scraping noise bouncing around the dark tavern hall. They hadn't even lit a fire. They were just eating and drinking themselves stupid. They didn't have any direction.

"Why are you harassing these rodents?" Jab demanded. "You should be ashamed of yourselves, deserting Nasalid only to become bandits."

Brouglas groaned, and Jab realized how much he'd overstepped.

The biggest squirrel of the group, a brute with more scars than teeth, grimaced and stomped over to them. "Ashamed? How does a wet sod know so much? And where are you from with that accent?"

Jab wished he still had his crossbow, more to display it than to use it. "I was a scout for Nasalid and washed ashore with my friend. We came here for shelter and heard that some of Nasalid's deserters were here."

The squirrel loomed over Jab. "You say his name as if you're not disgusted by him. You're kissing his hindpaws?" The bandit unsheathed a scimitar, the only thing about him that seemed polished and taken care of.

Brouglas pushed Jab aside. "Now wait, you. He is a child. You do not make threats. He sorry for mean words."

"Freng barbarian?" the bandit leader spat. The other five thugs came beside him, and he lifted his scimitar, pointing it at the beaver. "Keep that tongue in your mouth before I cut it out."

"Leave town," Brouglas said. "We don't want trouble."

Jab's heart quickened. Brouglas didn't have a sword or armor. He and Jab barely had a full set of clothes between the two of them. These were all armed and armored rodents, and none of them were in a good mood.

"You walked into it," the big one said.

"Jab, get high," Brouglas said in Frenglese. He slapped his tail against the floor, drawing the attention toward him, which made enough noise for the tapestries to rustle again. His words were simple enough for Jab to understand.

Jab pulled back a step, then jumped onto the wall, digging in with his paws, latching onto the soft wood. Jab had to trust him. If nothing else, the bigger squirrels would be too big and weighed down with armor to climb after him. As Jab climbed, he noticed the chandelier above, hanging from the ceiling by a metal chain, all seven candles extinguished. Below him, the leader lunged at Brouglas.

The beaver sidestepped and caught the blade between his ribs and the inside of his arm, holding it by his armpit. He swung his hips and knocked the scimitar from the leader's grasp and then took it into his free paw.

The other squirrels drew their scimitars and closed in on him. "Somebody go after the kid!" the big one shouted.

Jab might've been a kid according to his age, but the death of his parents and the battles he'd survived had forged him into something else. He scurried toward the chandelier, barely latching on to the rafters with his claws, thankful for his light weight and all the training he'd done as a scout. His shoulders and arms burned, but he had to get to that fixture. Below, Brouglas parried the strikes of four of the squirrels, grunting and hissing as he struggled to match pace.

Jab would've never imagined praying that a bunch of Grovekeepers had drunk too much fermented berry juice and would lose a fight to a Sprouter, but here he was. The fifth deserter, the smallest of the group, had stripped his armor and begun climbing the wall after Jab, scimitar clenched between his teeth. Age, weight, and the berry juice seemed to be slowing him and weakening his grip, but Jab couldn't press his luck. The chandelier could trap at least one of the attackers if it fell at the right time.

But as Brouglas sank to a knee, Jab knew it wouldn't be enough. Arms screaming at him, Jab turned around and raced toward his own pursuer.

As the deserter reached the corner of the wall and ceiling, Jab swung himself off the rafter, catapulting himself toward him.

The deserter's eyes widened and his mouth dropped while he paused just long enough for Jab to grab the scimitar's exposed handle. The pursuer fell to the floor. It wouldn't be enough of a drop to kill him, but it would definitely take him out of commission. He hit with a thud and gasp.

As Jab fell himself, he struck the nearest tapestry with his scimitar, ruining the blade and slowing his descent.

The other attackers wheeled on Jab and their fallen comrade. Jab hopped off the tapestry and landed on his pursuer's chest. Brouglas was still breathing.

Jab sucked in air, then let the scimitar hover over the deserter's face. "You'll stop this right now. You call yourselves Grovekeepers? Read the Divine Poetics. We're supposed to treat Sprouters and Mulchers with kindness." He wondered how he could call himself a Grovekeeper, holding a blade over someone's face.

The big one who still hadn't reclaimed his scimitar lumbered forward. "Nasalid is a poison. That's why we left. There's n-nothing you can do to make us leave."

Jab pointed at the window. A crowd had formed outside, with Gizlee and Yumruk at the front, peering in. "Go ahead and kill a child while they watch. If the Sprouters are as evil as you say, they'll stab you in the back the first chance you get. Leave this place and come with me back to Qawar. You might not like the Liberator, but if you really believed your own lies, you wouldn't have come to Coppergrass to hurt innocent people and drink fermented berry juice." Some part of Jab was mad at Yumruk for not helping them with his crossbow, but he supposed this would've been much bloodier if he had.

The middle-sized squirrel among them threw his scimitar down. "The kid has a point. We shouldn't have touched that drink."

The second largest stepped away in the other direction. "Kid, don't hurt our friend. We'll leave."

"Pellets to that," the big one hissed, jerking his head at the two who'd spoken up. "Nothing's waiting for us in Qawar. They'll hang us for d-deserting."

Jab stepped off the unconscious one. "That's not true. You'll come back with us. Nasalid will want to know what you learned in Coppergrass and he'll want to see me again."

One of the scouting rules Jab had learned was to make lies sound honest if caught by the enemy. He hated it, but it had already saved his life twice. He wished it had been harder to lie. He had no clue if Nasalid wanted to see him again, but he didn't know what else to say. Too much berry juice or not, these squirrels *would* kill Brouglas.

Lines of scarlet streaked the beaver's fur.

"The Liberator made it nice and clear what the price of desertion was," the big one said, whiskers drooping. His breath stank.

Grunting, Brouglas brought himself to stand, and huffed out a few words in Frenglese. "Boy, I can't think clear enough ... for your language," he said between heavy breaths. "Tell them, say sorry to the townsrodents, and ask if they can live here as guardians. Defenders."

Jab nodded, but if this place didn't already have guards, it must be too peaceful to need them. Something must have changed. "Why did you come here? Where were the town guards?"

The mid-sized one picked up his dropped scimitar and sheathed it. "The new mayor sent them to the capital. This place was undefended."

Then Jab would have some words for this new mayor, and he imagined Gizlee would too. "How about you apologize to the innocent rodents outside and offer to replace the guards they lost? We're keeping these two scimitars."

The other three squirrels who still had their weapons nodded. The big one grunted. "Get that new mayor out here and we'll bargain."

"We'll go there together with the townsrodents," Jab said. "Can you help me get your friend off the floor?"

Still breathing heavily, Brouglas leaned over so Jab could see him, and he flashed a big smile before opening the door, letting Gizlee and Yumruk inside.

12

SANU

Under the Gnaverwood's canopy, we will know victory against these foul invaders.

- General Ironseed's speech
before the Battle of Batina

The sailing cog fleet moored in the harbor outside a port city on Coppergrass Isle. Based on the shoreline, Sanu assumed this was the island's east side, the coast closer to Qawar. The city's docks could only accommodate one ship, which naturally was reserved for Ridgerd's.

From Sanu's perspective, it seemed as if the other ships could've been disassembled and the planks laid all side by side and stretched wider than the city. Accompanying Ridgerd felt wrong, but that might've been because Yagub walked a few paces back, chatting with Nett. Sanu wondered if *he* had been like that trying to talk with Cladh back in ZelZaytun, but he shook his head at the ridiculous thought.

He didn't have any romantic feelings for Cladh, he just liked spending time with her and considered whether it would be acceptable for a squirrel and hamster to marry. In a hypothetical sense, of course.

Ridgerd's shadow passed over Sanu, and he peered around the colossal man, watching Lady Marjitay and the Sapling Galdwin march off the exit plank. Trumpeters strode out in front, holding flags with Ridgerd's hawk symbol and others with stylized Ganan Rakes. He was glad nobody had a banner or flag for Lady Marjitay though she honked obnoxiously enough that she didn't quite need one. He hoped all mole rats weren't like her.

A crowd had gathered at the dock, giving Sanu a fresh memory of arriving in Freng last week. Learning the person they'd come to deliver a message to had died and interrupting his funeral wasn't something Sanu wanted to repeat. Sanu wondered what else he could possibly be stepping in, but at least he was with a king this time.

He would've preferred having his brother though. A piece of him knew Jab was alive somewhere, but the Great Sea was so vast, with so many islands, he could have washed up anywhere.

With Yagub too far behind, Sanu had nobody left except the king. Sanu glanced up at him, and the way he stared into the distance made him seem lonely too.

"Where are we?" Sanu asked.

"Coppergrass Isle. The map says this is Newhouse City. They have good olive cakes from what I hear." King Ridgerd scrunched his whiskers. "Sorry, you probably aren't allowed to eat that, are you?"

"My brother would know for sure, but I'm guessing not." Sanu furrowed his brow. He'd seen maps of Coppergrass Isle and distinctly remembered a city named ZelNuhas. Maybe Ridgerd couldn't pronounce it, since that was a Qawari name.

"Is this island part of your kingdom?" Sanu asked.

"Mine?" Ridgerd asked. "No. My cousin rules here. We'll get a warm welcome and our ships' storm damage will be repaired." As they walked down the plank, Ridgerd gestured at the other ships, all of which had sustained damage in the storms, with torn sails and holes in the hulls. Two had broken prows, and Sanu wasn't sure how that could've happened.

Not that he questioned it.

He'd welcome any delay to the invasion of his home. He didn't want soldiers descending on Qawar. A sick feeling twisted his gut. Maybe there was some way he could ruin these ships, or at least sink a few. When nobody was looking and everyone was off the ships, maybe he could sneak inside and start a fire or something.

But another part of him didn't like the idea of betraying Ridgerd. If it weren't for him, Lady Marjitay would've had Sanu killed by now. Though maybe Ridgerd only wanted Sanu alive because Sanu could be useful to him. Not very heroic.

Sanu averted his gaze from the king, and the sky seemed like the only thing that wasn't conflicted anymore.

As they disembarked, Sanu could make out the banners of the welcoming group. These sigils had Ganan's Rake on them, but it seemed tiny compared to the symbol in the center. Where Ridgerd's entourage appeared excited, these other ones on the dock looked annoyed by the way they shifted.

Ridgerd's trumpeters blared the king's arrival with a bright brass fanfare. A muscular porcupine lowered his instrument and called out in a sing-song voice that reminded Sanu of the call to prayer back home. "You stand in the presence of King Ridgerd, newly ascended over his late father Hedgry, the youngest ruler in Freng and leader of the great reclamation army."

A mole rat stepped forward, allowing Sanu a chance to see the image on the banner clearly. Standing over a small Ganan's Rake was either a ram or a goat, yet the horns looked peculiar. Sanu edged closer and realized the animal's horns were shaped like crossbows. It reminded him of Lady Marjitay's goose and crossbow sigil, and not in a pleasant way.

Ridgerd stiffened and stopped in his tracks, shaking the plank. "Something is wrong," he muttered.

The mole rat blew his trumpet, and the squeak which followed sounded more like noise than music. With forced enthusiasm, the mole rat straightened. "Her grace, Lady Bohbrat, welcomes you to Coppergrass Isle, and the mayor, her daughter, welcomes you to Newhouse City, the proud trading port on the eastern side of the island. The mayor will receive you in the grand mansion." He turned to the side, taking stock of the Sapling and Lady Marjitay. "Please bring all delegates, both royal and holy, with you."

"What's the matter?" Sanu caught himself from finishing his question to Ridgerd with "my king."

"That isn't my cousin's sigil, and I've never heard of this Bohbrat. Something dark has happened to Coppergrass Isle." His paw hovered near the sword at his waist. "Keep close to me. We're walking into danger."

Sanu cast an eye back at the fleet of ships he wanted to sink and then at the royal hamster who promised to keep him safe. Sanu felt like he had two hearts. One which wanted to search for clues about Jab, and another to do everything in his power to sabotage the invasion. Both felt wrong.

13

JAB

Yes, there are situations in which you may resort to violence. There are situations in which spouses may divorce. Permitting something regrettable does not mean I wish you to seek unfortunate last resorts. Strive to improve relationships before severing them.

- Divine Poetics

Jab's new scimitar weighed heavily on his belt, dragging down his clothes that were barely dried and still stank like the sea. He'd won a fight without throwing a punch, yet knowing he'd threatened another rodent's life, a Grovekeeper, no less, weighed more than the sword.

The cheering townsrodents of Rado Town and a happy Brouglas didn't do much to dilute his guilt, despite it all.

Jab eyed the smaller deserter, the one who'd first refused their leader. He seemed more like a reasonable rodent than the others, and knowing he'd deserted Nasalid turned Jab's stomach even more than his indulging in the forbidden fermented berry juice. Seeing how the other deserters mumbled and groaned about the light, Jab got a clearer idea of why the All-Planter commanded Grovekeepers to stay away from drinks like that. Maybe those rules weren't as random as he'd once thought.

Gizlee strode beside Brouglas, and she translated the townsrodents' compliments for him.

A petty part of Jab wondered where *his* thank-yous and compliments were. Maybe the crowd who'd peered inside the window and watched the scuffle hadn't looked up to see Jab's ceiling acrobatics. Or maybe they fawned on the beaver knight because he was a Sprouter. Jab wondered where the town's Grovekeepers were. Maybe all Coppergrass's rodents with Qawari ancestry were Sprouters. Jab didn't like being in the same group as the deserters, with nobody else to represent their faith, and he definitely didn't want to be lumped into a category with them.

He hoped Sanu was doing better than him.

The trip to the town mayor was blissfully short, even though Jab lost count of the number of houses they'd passed on the paved stone road.

Gizlee looked over her shoulder at Jab. "The mayor is a spiny mouse. Have you ever met one, young hero?" Her whiskers twisted a little as she smiled. She really was beautiful in a way that few adults were. Something about her demeanor was inspiring, but it was more than her good looks. Her voice was both kind and firm, her posture both strong and confident. Jab could envision her as a real leader of rodents. And with a big oaf like Yumruk and his crossbow by her side, it was easy to imagine few would question her.

The mayor's mansion, if it could be called that, stood a few feet taller than the other homes, but did not reach higher than the prayer house, the Gananshed.

Gizlee sighed, and motioned to Yumruk, who knocked. His fist shook the pine door hard enough that Jab got angry all over again at the mole rat for staying away from the earlier fight. As Jab watched him, he tried to let that resentment go. It was what the All-Planter would want. Being physically large and knowing how to use a weapon did not mean that someone should fight or should even want to. Being angry at Yumruk for not fighting felt similar to despising the deserters.

A gerbil answered the door, dressed like the other locals and just as gaunt. He stood and spoke as if all joy and enthusiasm had left him, words falling out in the mishmash language that blended Qawari and Frenglese. Jab could only guess at the meaning, but he was decently sure he caught words meaning "mayor," "not," and "seeing." Whatever he said, at the sight of the deserters and the crowd behind them, the depressed gerbil straightened. He asked a question in a demanding tone, and Jab guessed he was asking what was the meaning of this, or something close to it.

Jab would've enjoyed puzzling this out more if he weren't still out of breath from the fight. But he wasn't about to get too far from his protector, so he eased past the deserters and joined Brouglas, getting a view of the inside.

Gizlee folded her arms, and she spoke in their language, but it was easier for Jab to understand when she spoke it. "Bring the mayor out. The town he's sworn to protect must speak with him."

Somehow, listening to her helped Jab appreciate bits of the language as he patched in his knowledge of Frenglese and his mother tongue. Maybe that was what was so enchanting about her.

When the door gerbil stuttered, Yumruk grunted.

A muffled voice sounded from inside, and Jab peered into the building for the source. The structure was darker than it should've been, like someone forgot to build windows or put lamps inside.

Gizlee stood on her tiptoes and put a paw to the side of her mouth. "Get out here," she shouted. "The bandits surrendered. We brought them here for your inspection."

The gerbil backed away, and he seemed relieved.

From the shadows of the mayor's home, a figure emerged, a little taller than Jab and shorter than the others. His clothes resembled the other townsrodents in style, yet the colors were brighter, as if these clothes hadn't known much outside work in the dirt. An ornate crossbow was strapped to his back, and it seemed more expensive than what Yumruk carried, and much larger than what Jab had used a few months ago when scouting for Nasalid. It seemed too unwieldy for anyone to use, but he remembered Lady Marjitay using a similar one to murder a holy man back in ZelZaytun, so he didn't want to underestimate this person.

This was the spiny mouse. His fur collected in points across his body, and Jab wondered if that was a trait of his species or something intentional like when Mulchers wove twigs into their beards. He looked like he could've been Yagub's age, give or take a year. His big clothes didn't quite fit and the crossbow was clearly meant for someone larger, giving him a comical appearance of one who was trying too hard.

Gizlee said something which Jab didn't understand, and then realized it was a name. "Hunter Bohbrat, son of the baroness."

Jab couldn't tell if her voice carried disdain or pity.

The spiny mouse gazed at the crowd and responded in accented Frenglese. "Why are you here?"

"Two strangers solved your problem for you." Gizlee motioned for Yumruk, who brought the bandits forward. "These bandits have agreed to protect the town to replace the guards your mother demanded for her castle."

Hunter Bohbrat stared at his hindpaws, and the crossbow handle threatened to smack the back of his head. "I'll have to send them to her castle too."

Brouglas scoffed. "Is this Coppergrass hospitality?" The next thing he asked went over Jab's head, but he thought he caught the word for "innocent." Whatever he said, he wasn't pleased.

Hunter's whiskers drooped. "I don't have a choice."

"Aren't you in charge?" Gizlee asked, not switching to Frenglese. "These rodents need work. We need guards. They learned their lesson and want to repent."

The crowd of gerbils, hamsters, and mole rats behind Jab all wore dirty versions of Hunter's clothes. As they nodded along with Gizlee's words, Jab realized that was why she kept speaking in their language. She must believe they deserved to know what was happening.

"All fighters go back to defend the castle." Hunter's words came out like a chant he'd been forced to learn.

Jab stepped forward and formulated his best Frenglese. "What do you want?" He pointed at Hunter's chest in case he was getting words wrong. "Do you want to be a town king?"

"Mayor," Brouglas corrected in a kind whisper.

"Do you want to be mayor?" Jab asked.

Hunter gazed out at the crowd, and then back to Jab. "My mother gave me this job."

Brouglas folded his muscled arms over his chest. "Answer the lad's question."

"She gave it to me," Hunter repeated.

Gizlee closed the distance between them and placed a paw on his shoulder. "But did you ask for it? Was this how you wanted your life to go?"

Hunter pushed away a budding tear. "I wanted to be an artist."

Jab's heart sank. He pitied this kid. Even though Hunter was older, he still felt like a teenager to Jab, way too young for this. The gold trim on his crossbow handle gave Jab an idea.

"Then stop being a mayor," Jab said. "My friend and I need to get to Qawar. Pay for our sailing there."

"Passage," Brouglas corrected.

"Our ... passage and come with us," Jab continued. "Qawar is home to many great artists. Then you won't have to deal with this job."

"My mom will find out," Hunter mumbled.

"And what'll she do if you're in Qawar?" Brouglas asked. "Come back—"

Hunter put a paw on the door. "Just leave me alone." He inclined his head to peer over Brouglas and Gizlee. "Go home, everyone."

Gizlee wiggled her nub of a tail. "What if we didn't? And what if *you* didn't? Take the boat. Let us deal with your mother." She leaned in close to him and whispered something. His eyes widened, and he stepped aside.

"I hereby leave Gizlee in charge. Please don't tell my mom." He looked at Jab. "I'll pay for a boat back to Qawar. Thank you. Just let me get my things."

The gerbil door attendant sighed, mumbled "thank you" to Gizlee, and waved her inside.

Some townsrodents cheered, and Jab tugged on Brouglas's elbow. "What did she whisper to him?"

The beaver knight slapped the dirt behind him with his tail. "I'm not sure I should repeat it, lad." His voice dropped to a whisper. "She warned him about what will happen if people want justice for what his mother did."

Jab tensed, wondering what kind of mother would deprive her son of protection. In the months since his parents died, he barely had time to grieve for them. He couldn't imagine what kind of person this Baroness Bohbrat was or what she did to get in power, but if it left a vacuum for a pawful of bandits to take over a whole town, it couldn't have been anything good.

14

SANU

When nations of Qawar and the surrounding islands know peace with Freng, we will commence trade and prosper as brothers united. I would invite all the kings and even the Arborist in Gananshire to pray in ZelZaytun's splendor.

- Excerpt from Nasalid the Liberator's message to the Frenglese kings.

Leaving Newhouse City's port, Sanu marched down stony streets alongside Ridgerd, with Yagub and Nett close behind. Something about being in the busy city and off the ship made the two teens stop their whispers and giggles, which Sanu appreciated, and it seemed like the king did as well. Lady Marjitay and Sapling Galdwin muttered to each other off to the side, which made Sanu's stomach turn.

The thought of her walking free still shook him to his core. Maybe Sprouters had a different system of justice for the wealthy. Jab would have something to say about that.

And he will, Sanu promised himself. He *would* see Jab again, and they'd complain about Lady Marjitay and find reasons to talk about Cladh and Qala, not that either of them liked either girl, and they'd tell each other about what they'd done while the other was away.

They'd be a family. They'd be brothers, reunited once again.

The trumpeters for Baroness Bohbrat lead the group to a large tavern, nestled in between a bakery and a gem merchant.

Sanu tugged at his whiskers, pondering. This must be a wealthy town to have both of those. No poor city would have a jewel merchant. He felt bad to be somewhere nice while Jab was who-knows-where.

But he *was* somewhere, Sanu reminded himself.

Ridgerd's banner carrier stopped at the tavern entrance, holding open the door for the king. As they passed, Ridgerd got in the porcupine's ear and whispered loud enough for Sanu to hear. "If there's even an idea of danger in your head, do not hesitate."

The porcupine nodded grimly. Maybe he was more than someone to carry around a flag and play an instrument.

Lady Marjitay huffed. "This isn't the mayoral mansion. I want to see the mayor."

"We're waiting for her here, *lady*," Ridgerd said. "We need to wait for a formal explanation of why my cousin is no longer in power, so we might as well enjoy the local food. I'm in need of a new poison tester. I'll make your food for you myself."

The mole rat narrowed her eyes. "Joke all you want, but you're paying for my meal."

"Mine as well," Galdwin said, smirking.

Sanu glared at the pair of them. He didn't care if they saw him at this point. It wasn't like they could throw him into prison again.

Ridgerd nodded somberly, and stepped inside the tavern. In a deep, resounding voice that put his trumpeter to shame, Ridgerd announced, "Friends, King Ridgerd bids you all hello and I am eager to try your best foods. My two regal companions here have nobly insisted on fasting to further imitate our gracious Lord Ganan, Blest be Him."

A few patrons at the tables raised their glasses and echoed, "Blest be Him." Once the reality of a king entering set in, the same patrons whispered to each other with widened eyes.

Marjitay and Galdwin fought scowls while finding seats.

Smiling at their discomfort, Sanu couldn't help but wonder what would happen if *he* were to get on the king's bad side.

A wizened red squirrel hobbled over, sporting a set of twigs entwined in his beard. This was a Mulcher, running a tavern. Maybe Sanu really had seen everything in the Great Sea now. The squirrel spoke in a language that sounded like a mix of Frenglese and Qawari. "Welcome to the

Busted Acorn. It is an honor to serve royalty. Please, take our finest table."

"Thank you," Ridgerd said, following the squirrel. "Say, do you have a double siege board and set? I heard you play it here more than the Qawari."

"Ah!" the Mulcher said, holding a finger up. "We have several sets. I'll fetch my finest and have my son bring you some water."

"Excellent, my good squirrel," Ridgerd replied, letting his voice fill the crowded room. Grumbling, Lady Marjitay and Sapling Galdwin took a seat at a different table. The king waved at Yagub and Nett for them to join him and Sanu.

They did, but Yagub seemed pleased, while Nett was scowling.

Sanu wondered what happened to Yagub, whether he was lovesick over Nett, a girl he barely knew, or starstruck over the king who saw him as a tool. The thought gripped Sanu for a moment, but he shook it off. Ridgerd wasn't like that. Rodents weren't objects to him. At least Sanu hoped they weren't.

Nett tsked. "They'll betray you, my king. And I should remind you that I don't only work for you. I am tasked to work for Sapling Galdwin as well."

The hamster king smiled as a young red squirrel brought over steins of water. He barely had the chin hairs to grow a beard, but Sanu noticed a single twig rolled into his hairs.

"These are from my father," the red squirrel said. "He wants to know what the king would like to eat."

Sanu appreciated the young man's politeness toward a king he didn't swear allegiance to. It was something he was hoping he was doing himself.

King Ridgerd drummed his fingers against the table. "What's something a rodent can only get on Coppergrass Isle? That is the meal I'd like."

The owner's son nodded. "And does the king understand I must make it according to my customs? As a Mulcher, I cannot make it with olive as some other rodents on this island would. This part of the city used to have more Grovekeepers come here, so it usually isn't an issue."

Yagub's eyes widened and Nett's scowl turned to a smirk.

The hamster reached up to place a gentle paw on the waiter's bicep. For Ridgerd's size, he could've picked him up by the arm. "I'm in enough trouble with the All-Planter already. I won't add to my list of sins by asking you to violate your beliefs. Make it your way, which is even better, I'm sure."

"'Good king Ridgerd,' indeed," Nett agreed.

"I was hoping for some olives though," Yagub muttered.

Sanu rolled his eyes. "I wouldn't have eaten the stuff with olives either."

The owner returned, carrying a polished oak case in his paw. "For the king, this double siege set has been in my family for generations. I would be honored if you played a game on it."

"And you honor me with your hospitality," Ridgerd replied. "Yagub, care for a round? This will pass the time until the new mayor greets us."

Disappointment wriggled in Sanu's stomach. He loved double siege. It was the only game he could beat Jab at and one of the last things he did with Dad before he died.

Yagub cast a half-second glance at Nett before shrugging. "My liege, I'm embarrassed to say I don't know how to play."

"Yes he does. Everyone from Qawar knows." Sanu beamed as realization dawned. "He's afraid to lose to you in front of Nett."

Nett chuckled and Yagub's cheeks reddened.

"Ha!" Ridgerd slapped the table, making the oak container bounce. "Then *you'll* be my adversary? I won't take it easy on you."

"I was about to say that to you."

Yagub and Nett's jaws dropped, which made the moment even better.

"If you're so confident," Ridgerd said as he opened the container, "then you'll allow me first move."

Sanu always let Jab go first. It was part of his winning strategy. All the good players knew going first was a disadvantage. "Of course."

The hamster unlatched the wood box and arranged the pieces between them. Sanu grabbed the open box and found the inside had an inlay of the playing board, and had two more hooks inside so it could be unfolded. Sanu let his paw glide over the nice finish. He'd never seen so much craftwork in something as unnecessary as a double siege board.

Even the pieces Ridgerd arranged were beautiful, more sculptures than simple figures. The four red villager pieces went into Sanu's corner and the four blues into Ridgerd's. Six soldier pieces made a ring around them, with one general piece each, two vanguard pieces, the unconstructed siege engines, and the castle wall pieces.

Sanu arranged his castle pieces in the traditional fashion, protecting the general piece and the vanguards. As he completed the arrangement, he looked to his opponent's side of the board. Ridgerd had built the castle around the villager pieces, leaving the general exposed.

Sanu's eyes widened. Ridgerd had said he wouldn't take it easy on Sanu, and here he was pawing him the victory before the first move. Maybe he thought the mayor would show up soon.

"Are you ready?" Ridgerd asked. "In Freng, we shake paws before we play as a sign of trust and sportsrodentship."

"In Qawar, we bow," Sanu said, arms folded.

"*Shake his paw,*" Yagub hissed.

Nett groaned. "Men."

Ridgerd retracted his paw and grinned. "I win, you shake my paw. You win, I bow to you. Deal?"

Sanu returned the grin and nodded.

Ridgerd made the first move, advancing the general five spaces forward.

Sanu couldn't believe what a buffoon this king was. He tried to keep the shock from his face as he studied the king. Had rodents let him win his whole life? Had he never really needed to learn how to play?

"That's your move?" Sanu asked.

"Ah, yes. The serious players in Freng will knock the table when they finish their turn, and

I forgot." Ridgerd's light knuckle tap against the table rattled the pieces.

Sanu sighed. This would be over faster than it took to set it up, which was a shame, since his favorite part was when the siege engines came out. Sanu grabbed a soldier piece and moved it forward toward Ridgerd's general. Sanu knocked.

Smiling, Ridgerd grabbed a vanguard piece and knocked over Sanu's soldier before pawing it to him and knocking. "One point for the king."

Sanu's eyes widened. He'd placed his soldier in the direct path of a vanguard, who didn't have to waste a turn leaving the castle because of Ridgerd's unusual setup. Sanu advanced another soldier, placing this one outside either vanguard's reach, but close enough to capture the general on the next turn. *Knock.*

Ridgerd captured the soldier with the general, exposing it again. *Knock.*

Blood pumping, Sanu advanced a third soldier toward the general. *Knock.* Ridgerd's general was so close to Sanu's troops that it would be over soon.

The second vanguard captured his third soldier. *Knock.*

Wincing, Sanu examined the pieces. He'd lost half his soldiers and Ridgerd's general was in striking distance of the castle. Sanu huffed. "I'll take my first build turn." He rotated the siege engine piece one quarter of the way and knocked.

Ridgerd advanced the general again, isolating the piece from the vanguard. *Knock.*

"My left vanguard is leaving the castle," Sanu said, bringing the piece in front of the wall. *Knock.*

The general advanced again, capturing the exposed vanguard. *Knock.*

Sanu's heart raced—this game wasn't over. Ridgerd couldn't win without siege engines, and Sanu's own general was still safe inside the castle. Sanu advanced his fourth soldier, putting it within striking distance of the vanguard. He anticipated that the hamster king would take the bait, allowing Sanu a chance to put his remaining vanguard on the wall to fire an arrow on a future turn.

"I'm taking my first build turn," Ridgerd announced, turning his siege piece halfway before knocking.

"But—" Sanu's protest fell short on his lips. The villagers were safe in the castle so they could work faster. That was a rule, but he'd never actually seen anyone use it. It just made more sense to put the general in the castle. Sanu shook his head and grabbed his vanguard. "I'm moving him to the wall." He placed the vanguard piece on the top slot and knocked.

"Wise." Ridgerd placed the general on Sanu's exposed soldier. He pawed it to Sanu and knocked.

Sanu had two soldiers left, one vanguard, and the general. "Second build action." Sanu rotated his siege engine piece another quarter turn and knocked.

"Good idea. So will I." Ridgerd placed his siege engine piece beside the castle and knocked.

Sanu stared at the board and his heart sank. "You'll win in two moves."

"I would've won this turn, but moving the vanguard to the wall was smart."

Sanu extended a paw. "Good game." He'd never seen anyone play like that. Risking the general was dangerous, but it worked. "Who taught you to play like that?"

Ridgerd smiled and shook Sanu's paw, gentler than he would've expected. "Battle. Nobles want glorious tales, but the average soldier wants to go home to their families. The general can draw attention to himself and save lives." He nodded his head in Marjitay and Galdwin's direction, both of whom were glowering into their drinks. "Besides, would you lose sleep over putting them in harm's way?"

"But even the general? You could lose."

"I'm familiar with the rules." Ridgerd twirled the general piece between his fingers. "I don't imagine the general as having anyone to go back to. All the general pieces in Freng have little Ganan Rakes on them. Our Mulcher friend's figure doesn't of course, but the idea is the same. Anyone who gives their life for Ganan's sake, Blest be Him, is guaranteed a spot in the Walled Garden. This general," he sighed and placed the piece back on the board, "would rather give his life on the battlefield than face the empty castle." Ridgerd straightened and his voice hardened. "That reminds me, I would know why my cousin isn't in the castle at this moment. Our game was fun, my friend, but the mayor's tardiness in receiving us is bothersome, to say the least."

Sanu's eyes widened. Stories of Ridgerd had reached Qawar, all of them detailing impossible feats, but one rumor remained constant: he'd never lost a fight. If he reached Qawar, the whole island would be doomed.

15

JAB

You told a student it would be impossible to reach the Walled Garden because of his failings, that he was doomed to the Droughtlands. Students' failures to learn belong to their teachers, so what shall the All-Planter say to you on Pruning Day?

- Raticenna's debate with a heretic

The goodbyes from the townsrodents were many and heartfelt. Gizlee bowed deeply to Brouglas and Jab, and gave a little more than a head bob in Hunter's direction, which was nicer than the mix of boos and scoffs from the crowd.

Watching Hunter's drooping whiskers and sagging tail stirred something in Jab. He wondered how Sanu would've been received back in Rattin if they'd known he'd spent time with Frenglese soldiers before Nasalid conquered ZelZaytun. It was a little pathetic to see Hunter like this, but Jab didn't know what to say to console someone older than him, so he said a prayer internally.

Gizlee sent the trio off with a basket of acorns that Yumruk picked and roasted. They left the town, headed for a place Hunter called Newhouse City, which sounded foreign yet distantly familiar.

He remembered reading over Sanu's shoulder once as Sanu pored over a map of their region of the Great Sea and seeing Coppergrass Isle. But their map couldn't have had a name as strange as "Newhouse." He was somewhat confident he'd seen a city named ZelNuhas, but maps were more Sanu's thing than Jab's back when their parents were still alive. In the All-Planter's sense of humor, Jab had been the one to assist with mapmaking for Nasalid.

A playful shove on his shoulder bolted Jab from his reflection.

"Lost in your thoughts, lad?" Brouglas chided.

Jab shook his head and responded in Frenglese. "Sorry. I was thinking about my brother."

"Aye," the beaver knight said. "I'm sure Sanu is thinking of you too. He did often back in the Holy City."

"Olihort?" Hunter asked. "You were in Olihort? What was the holy Gnaverwood like? I saw regular ones in Freng, but I heard the holy one in Olihort is the grandest."

Jab fought the urge to scowl. Olihort was the Sprouter name for ZelZaytun. But Hunter probably didn't know about Nasalid's liberation, and he wondered how much honest history Hunter had learned, based on what Jab was hearing about Hunter's mother.

The town faded behind them and the road narrowed. The grove of squat trees thickened to a forest around them.

"We both were in ZelZaytun," Brouglas answered. "On opposite sides of a siege, no less," he gave Jab another playful shove and a hearty laugh. "Though I can't say I'm disappointed it's no longer in Lady Marjitay's paws. She's a piece of work, that one."

Hunter sighed. "I know the type. I bet she'd like my mom."

At least Gizlee was nothing like those other women. Jab would've greatly preferred *her* on a throne to Lady Marjitay or Hunter's mom.

The road under their hindpaws gave way to chalky dirt, causing Jab to take note of their surroundings again. The nice houses were replaced by hovels and shacks. Behind them, red squirrels chopped at trees. Chains connected their ankles.

"Is this still part of the town?" Jab asked, checking over his shoulders. It seemed like this was a forgotten area.

The playfulness left Brouglas's voice. "Are these forced laborers?"

Hunter avoided their gaze, looking down. "It wasn't my idea."

A quick look to the sky told Jab it was nearly prayer time. The Divine Poetics said that if making prayer at the right time is impossible, to strive to do something virtuous. Jab stepped in front of him and made him stop. "What wasn't your idea? What's going on with them?"

Jab squinted at the red squirrels. The men were bearded, and their dress didn't quite match the townsrodents' garb. Looking more closely, he noticed tiny leaves attached to twigs protruding from their beards. These were Mulchers.

Brouglas folded his arms and leaned forward, and even Jab felt the size differential between them. "Answer his question."

Hunter scratched the back of his head. "They are cutting trees to make crossbow bolts. For my mom's garrison."

A chill ran down Jab's spine. "Why are they so thin? Why are they in shackles like this? Why chain them?"

"My mom brought them here from another part of the island." He stared at his hindpaws. "She told me to put them here."

"Have you paid them, lad?" Brouglas asked. He leaned in so close to the spiny mouse that he could've bit off a whisker.

"The ones who don't work get sent to the capital." Hunter's sigh came out like a wheeze. "I don't know what happens to them after."

A dark thought racked Jab's mind. "We aren't far from the town. What do the other rodents think?"

"They, um, they—"

Brouglas stepped back and unsheathed his new scimitar. "Lad, speak plain. We aren't playing now."

A tear slithered through Hunter's fur and wetted the cracked path. "I didn't tell them my mom wouldn't let me pay them."

"That's why you were willing to get on a boat to Qawar," Jab said. "You didn't want to face what you did when Gizlee found out. Your mom may have told you not to pay them, but you could have anyway." Jab pointed a stiff finger in the direction of town. "We aren't taking one more step forward until they know. This wood they're cutting can make new homes. If your mom is holed up in the capital, she won't know if they're allowed to go home free, will she?"

Hunter shook his head. "I can't leave my mom undefended. She needs the crossbow bolts to equip her soldiers."

Brouglas spat in the dirt. "Sounds like she's afraid of her own rodents. That's a bit pathetic, don't you think, lad? She must be quite unpopular here. You set these Mulchers free and you can make sure that legacy stays with her instead of your family."

"Pay them for all the work they've already done." Jab cast an eye skyward. He'd definitely missed the prayer time, and he hoped what he was trying to do would satisfy the All-Planter's commandment.

Hunter reached for his belt and grabbed an acorn pouch. "We need my money to pay for a boat."

Jab shook his head. "We'll find another way. Apologize, pay up, tell Gizlee, and we'll head back toward the city with the boat."

By now, some of the red squirrels had stopped working and were peeking around houses. It was here, Jab realized, how depressed they all seemed. The part of his brain that had tried to embody Sanu was screaming that these rodents should have revolted. But seeing how pathetic

Hunter was, Jab was glad they hadn't. The poor boy was a puppet for his master.

Hoofbeats clopped in the distance, and Hunter's eyes widened. "We have to go."

Brouglas pushed Hunter's shoulder, much harder than he had with Jab a few minutes ago. "No. Do as Sanu says."

Sanu?

Jab winced at the wrong name, but reminded himself that he would get confused for his twin often in life. The hoofbeats grew louder. Jab hadn't heard that many horses since the siege.

A band of five riders bounded up the road.

"No," Hunter whispered. "I'm so sorry."

"What?" Jab said, turning around.

The band rode past Jab and his companions, moving up the side of the lane between the shacks and the timber.

"I've dealt with bandits once already today," Brouglas hissed. "I don't fancy tangling with any more."

"Those aren't bandits," Hunter said.

Jab's paw fell toward his scimitar. "Who are they?"

"My mom's riders. They're collecting the wood early."

One rider strode up the lane. "Prince Hunter?" The rider grabbed his spear and pointed it at Brouglas. "And who are you, abducting the prince?" The language came in Frenglese, not the mishmash they'd heard in town.

The question came with spears, drawn and pointed at Jab and Brouglas's necks.

16

SANU

When I enlisted, I thought my sergeant was the cruelest squirrel in all the Great Sea. He drove us to the brink, insisting war would do worse, so we had better be prepared. Yet my squad became the most reliable group I'd ever known. It was the shared burden that bound us together. You may recognize my sergeant, for he was also the one who trained you. When the ruling council gave me control of this army, I dug him out of retirement. Learn from him like he's your grandparent.

- General Ironseed's reprimand to a failed sergeant.

Their meals came from the kitchen with the owner and his son, who placed food on the table in front of Ridgerd first, then Nett, and Yagub and Sanu last. The promised Coppergrass dish's nutty and pine aroma filled the air, and Sanu's stomach roared more than it had since he'd craved Mom's sheltercake. Realizing that he got his food while Lady Marjitay went hungry, made everything smell better too.

"Sapling Galdwin!" Ridgerd called. "Since you have elected to fast, it would honor us all if you led the blessing on our food."

The beaver narrowed his eyes. "It was made by Mulchers, so I don't have to."

The banner carriers and trumpeters at the other table stared wide-eyed.

"In fact, *my liege*," Galdwin hissed, "I'm shocked you'd eat anything here. It's quite profane."

The hamster's eyes narrowed, and under his breath, he retorted, "You say that about everything I do." Straightening, he stood and placed a paw on Sanu's shoulder. "Correct me if I'm wrong, dear Sapling, but was it not Ganan, Blest be Him, who miraculously purified rancid food? You can correct me on the story, but if memory serves, it was a plate of dark beans, much like what this fine gentlerodent has prepared for me, and this doesn't look bad at all, but fresh and scrumptious. Remind me of the dish's name?" He extended his paw toward the owner, and nodded with a grand smile.

The Mulcher bowed. "Thank you, good king. It's called loov."

"'Loov,'" Ridgerd repeated. "So, my gracious Sapling, if I keep the name of Ganan, Blest be Him, upon my lips, it can purify anything. Much like how you are fasting the entire *day* to purify your own heart from judgmental thoughts."

Sanu wondered if saying the name of a holy person was the best idea for making sure food was safe to eat. He didn't think shouting "All-Planter" would remove bird poop from food. He glanced around the table and found Nett and Yagub didn't appreciate the back-and-forth as much as Sanu had.

The hamster king motioned toward the food. "I thank the All-Planter for sending Ganan, Blest be Him, who sent the truth. I thank the chef who sent the food, and the plants and animals who provided. To a blessed meal!"

Sanu observed the other rodents in attendance raising their forks in the air, with the exception of the few Mulchers in the room, who bowed their heads. He wondered if their forks were somehow miniature representations of Ganan's Rake in their eyes, but he didn't want to ask. Yagub's eyes were on Nett, and Sanu wondered what had happened to his friend. Nett was nice, but he couldn't understand Yagub's infatuation. He hoped for a brief second he hadn't been looking at Cladh like that while in ZelZaytun. But of course, he hadn't. That would be silly.

As the toast ended, Nett shoved her fork into her food. "You are crossing the wrong people, my king."

"I'm only worried about crossing the All-Planter." The hamster dug a spoon into his loov and took a bite.

Yagub's mouth dropped. "You aren't testing it for poison?"

King Ridgerd waved his fork in a tight circle while pointing it at him. "My test is my nose.

I'm not sure if you had an overbearing mother, but imagine one with a queen's resources at her disposal." He sniffed the morsel, and the nutty aroma wafted over to Sanu. "Most poisons have a smell. The ones that don't discolor food. Any others are destroyed by cooking the food." He took a bite and winked at Yagub.

Sanu accepted this as his signal to start eating. The loov carried a sharp bite and it excited his stomach like he was breaking a fast. As he chewed, he realized that Jab would love this; they'd eat it together one day soon.

The doors to the tavern opened, but Sanu couldn't see around the king to get a good look at whoever entered.

As everyone else began eating, the owner hobbled over. "Does the king find it pleasing?"

Ridgerd grabbed a kerchief and dabbed the corners of his mouth. "No."

Sanu raised an eyebrow and Nett rolled her eyes.

As the Mulcher owner backed away with drooped whiskers, Ridgerd slammed his paw on the table. "Pleasing is too weak a word, my friend. I'll bring my chef to meet you. He'll learn this from you. Fetch me another."

A new voice broke in. "I'm afraid that's impossible." The interloper was the mole rat trumpeter who greeted them before. "Lady Gavrer is ready for you in the mayor's mansion."

Ridgerd took another hearty bite, pushing the food to the side of his cheek and puffing it out like a balloon. He motioned for Sanu to scoot down. "Sit with us, friend. Eat."

The trumpeter frowned. "King Ridgerd, I came to fetch you."

Behind him, Sapling Galdwin and Lady Marjitay approached.

Ridgerd sighed. "Nett and Yagub, I'm sure you two would love an expedition together. Return to the ship and bring the chefs here. Have the other crews disembark so the whole army might enjoy the delights of this city."

Galdwin tutted. "My liege, unloading an army in such a manner would be seen as an act of war. You do not wish for war on Coppergrass Isle."

"Of course I don't," Ridgerd said while chewing. "But perhaps unloading an army will hasten a response to my question about who is ruling and where my cousin is?" He gulped down his drink and cut his next bite. "I suppose asking a mayor to wait for a king would be an act of war also?"

"It's certainly insulting," Lady Marjitay said.

Sanu repressed the urge to shout "so is your face," but he kept it in check.

"Fine then. I wouldn't be so rude." Ridgerd motioned for the owner to come back over. "The Sapling here will pay for our meal as an apology for his unkind remarks about Mulchers. Sometimes he gets so twisted in philosophy he forgets pragmatics."

Sanu finished his meal faster than he would've liked. The beans and onions tasted so good he wished he could've stretched out the experience of eating it. He couldn't believe a king had to listen to rodents like this.

As Sir Galdwin grumbled and reached for his gold pouch, Ridgerd stood and motioned for the others at his table to do the same. He placed a wide hand on the trumpeter's shoulder. "Lead the way, my good man."

Outside, a carriage awaited with two regal white horses at the front. The trumpeter motioned toward it. "We prepared this for you, King Ridgerd."

"Ha!" Ridgerd walked over as his own trumpeter and banner carriers hurried beside him. He stood beside the carriage and pointed to its carved wood roof. "Do you think I could fit in such a small contraption? And if you can't carry me and my whole entourage, I won't ride while they walk." He gestured to the buildings around them. "I want to experience Newhouse City. Allow me to smell this beautiful place and see the wonderful rodents in it as we walk. Surely, Mayor ... Gavrer, was it? Surely, she wouldn't expect me to speed away in a carriage by myself without my men at my side."

Yagub's eyes widened, and Sanu understood his emotion this time. Being one of Ridgerd's "men" felt prestigious. For such a giant and charismatic hamster to find some lowly squirrel worthy of manhood, felt empowering.

"Allow Lady Marjitay to ride." The king opened the door and motioned for her. "Since you decided to fast, you must be feeling weak. Please ride. Your king requests it."

The mole rat grumbled before entering the carriage, and Ridgerd assisted her in a way that almost seemed kind.

Once inside, the mole rat stuck her head out the window. "Permit the Sapling to ride with me. He also must be tired after you declared he was fasting."

As she finished speaking, Galdwin stepped out of the inn, carrying a noticeably smaller coin pouch. "I am quite tired from fasting."

Ridgerd's eye twitched.

Sanu nudged Yagub. "There's enough room in there for you too," he whispered. "Go inside."

"What?" Yagub whispered back.

"Ridgerd wants to be able to watch what those two are doing. By putting them together in a closed carriage, they could plot something."

Nett poked her head around from Yagub's side. "He won't be safe alone." The porcupine grabbed Yagub by the wrist and stood before the king. "My liege, let us join them. I need to divide my time between you and the Sapling."

Ridgerd glanced down at Sanu and winked, then hailed the mayor's trumpeter. "Surely, you could fit two more in there? I have the Sapling's assistant and one of my guardsrodents here who can join them." Ridgerd pulled the door open for the Sapling and peered inside. "Yes, there's enough room. Come on, you two, enjoy the ride. Listen to everything you can about this fine settlement. As for me, I shall walk together with my friends."

Once Yagub and Nett entered, the carriage lurched forward as the driver urged on the horses.

The trek through Newhouse allowed Sanu to appreciate the city's architecture. Growing up, he mostly ignored buildings' appearances, but after his time in the Holy City, the majesty of buildings drew him in. These buildings sported domes like in ZelZaytun and in Rattin, but they had Ganan's Rakes on top of them like in Freng.

He scanned the streets for signs of Grovekeepers, but aside from a bakery that sold sheltercakes, he couldn't find any. One building looked like it might have been a prayer hall, but the spot where the Grovekeeper symbol would have been was bare. He wasn't sure what the Mulchers called their holy buildings, but he felt like he would've known one if he'd seen it.

"Admiring the city?" Ridgerd asked, breaking Sanu from his architectural trance.

"Oh, yes. I was hoping to see some Grovekeepers here."

Ridgerd scratched his chin. "That is odd. Coppergrass Isle is famous in Freng. It's always been a place where the three great faiths lived peaceably."

Sanu nodded, debating if he should add that Qawar was like that too ... until the Frenglese invaders came during his grandparents' time. He decided against it, since Ridgerd's grandfather led the invasion. "So where are they then?"

"That's a good question. I'd like to know, myself."

Sanu breathed deep. "You don't hate Grovekeepers, right?"

The hamster arched an eyebrow. "You're the only Grovekeeper I've had much contact with, and you're a delight. I'm sure you have both the virtuous and the villainous, like with Sprouters."

Sanu fought the urge to clench his fist. "Then why invade Qawar? Lots of Grovekeepers will die if you do."

Tearing his gaze from Sanu, Ridgerd exhaled a deep sigh. "Such is the reality of war. I wish there were another way. But all those rodents on my ship? They believe retaking the Holy City will allow them into the Walled Garden. It might do that for me too. Or at least keep me from the Droughtlands."

"But why would you go to the Droughtlands? You're a good king."

"Thank you," Ridgerd said after a mirthless laugh. "Sapling Galdwin and Lady Marjitay know what kind of a rodent I am. My father did too. If they are right, then all hope might be lost for me." A sadness infused the king's voice that Sanu didn't understand.

"Is it because you play pranks on them? Like with the fasting?"

"No." Ridgerd brought his weary gaze back to Sanu, then tore it away. "I am as the All-Planter made me. But in the eyes of many, being who I am means being destined for the Droughtlands."

Sanu's eyes drifted to Ridgerd's giant sword. "A fighter, you mean? Because the All-Planter made you huge and good in a fight?"

"Let's go with that. The All-Planter gave me my size, but it's my father who molded me into a fighter. Supplying the garrison at Castle Kraksnout to keep Lady Marjitay on her throne while he warmed his own was my father's crowning achievement. All the Frenglese nations are supposed to supply the Olihort soldiers, but none did more than my father."

Sanu's tail stiffened. "You're waging a war because of him, aren't you? You're trying to live up to his expectations."

Some of Ridgerd's mirth returned. "With a mind as sharp as yours, I'm impressed with myself even more for beating you in double siege. And I promise, I'm not. I couldn't satisfy him in life, so I doubt I can in death. My hope is to arrive in Qawar with an unstoppable army, and Nasalid will surrender without a fight, which would be my preference. So many of the seedlings I had to bring despise me because they listen to the Sapling. And that boat we lost had most of the soldiers who hate me too."

Bitter bile rose in Sanu's throat. "The last time a Frenglese army came over, all the people of ZelZaytun were slaughtered."

"Not very knightly," Ridgerd replied. "I would not allow my soldiers to act in such a way. We're warriors of the All-Planter, not some shirt less Mausfjord raiders. And you should know my grandfather fought against that particular decision."

Cloppa

The carriage sped away, startling the trumpeter and banner carriers.

"What?" Ridgerd demanded. "Why are they speeding ahead?"

The king's trumpeter stopped in his tracks. "I don't know. They have some reason to get to the mayor first."

"That's not good," Ridgerd said. He turned to the banner carrier and Sanu. "We're running to catch up. Treachery is afoot."

As Sanu pursued the royal hamster, he noticed a single Grovekeeper prayer hall with the windows bashed in. His blood ran cold. This was *not* a safe place.

17

JAB

- Divine Poetics

In a thicket of stubby citrus trees, iron manacles clamped on Jab's wrists, and a steel spear hovered near his face.

Jab mustered his best Frenglese. "We are Hunter's friends. He—" Jab jerked his head in Brouglas's direction, "—is knight."

The beaver struggled against his own manacles. "The spiny mouse was escorting us to passage off the island."

Hunter's gaze fell to his hindpaws. "Um, they kidnapped me. Rado Town isn't safe for me now. I can't go back there."

"What?" The lead rider, a gopher, dismounted and trudged up to Brouglas. The gopher back-pawed Brouglas with his iron gauntlet, impacting the beaver's cheek. Something cracked.

Grunting, the beaver knight spat out a molar. "He speaks false. The boy was escaping his own mother. For her to hire scum like you, I understand why."

"Hmpf." The gopher shook his wrist. "We'll see what Baroness Bohbrat says about that."

Jab shuddered, beholding the rider's metal armor. He'd seen Sir Brouglas in full armor once, and he'd seen other Frenglese soldiers parade about in their suits, but what this one wore was something else entirely. A blackened covering of interlocked chains was worn as an undershirt, covered by a vest of metallic scales with a black cape attached at the shoulders, the fabric, a quilt of blackened bird feathers.

It must've been even more unbearably hot than the clunky getups the Frenglese fighters wore, but it did create an intimidating image. He wondered if they were intentionally dressing like the owl-demons from Grovekeeper lore. It certainly wouldn't surprise him to learn these riders gobbled up children.

"Hunter," Jab pleaded, "tell the truth."

The spiny mouse shook his head. "I did." His gaze turned to the lead rider. "Please let them go. Don't hurt them."

"Your mother needs to hear about this," the gopher retorted. He snorted derisively and pointed at the toiling Mulchers in the distance who seemed oblivious to their scuffle. "Are these dirt farmers?"

Jab couldn't figure out what he meant by "dirt farmer," but it felt like a hateful thing to call the Mulchers.

Brouglas snorted, slapping his tail against the dirt. "That's rich. You ever heard of a beaver who is a Mulcher?"

The lead rider smacked him again. "That's enough outta you. The baroness will decide what to do with you three."

"Why me?" Hunter asked.

"Because you either got captured or are running away. Those are two things your mom pays me to prevent." He reached into his chain mail shirt, which must have had a slit Jab couldn't see, and he pulled out another pair of manacles. "You'll be safe with me. We'll go at a walking pace."

Another rider yanked on Jab's manacles, making him stumble. As Jab regained his footing, he noticed a younger Mulcher worker had stopped working and was staring at them. Jab and the child held eye contact for a few precious seconds before Jab was shoved in the back, forcing him forward. At the same moment, a paw appeared on the Mulcher kid's neck, pulling him back to work.

He wondered how Sanu was faring on the boat, and if they'd reached Qawar yet. But some part of him knew that Sanu was searching for him.

Walking forward in manacles wasn't as bad as knowing a cart full of wood taken from enslaved Mulchers was being pulled behind them. Jab stared at his hindpaws as they marched, following the sad swerving line of Brouglas's tail in front of him. He couldn't believe Hunter had betrayed them. He'd thought Hunter was just a sad teenager navigating complicated issues with his mom.

Jab tried to clench his fist, but the manacles pinched too tightly. Jab wasn't like Hunter. He was dealing with the trauma of losing a parent in a better way—helping others. He told himself he never would act like Hunter, but he wondered where he would've been without Nasalid's scout corps and Nasalid's personal direction. He'd needed that time with the hero to fully understand the importance of a positive older rodent in his life. Mom had been great, but maybe because she was Jab's own mother, Jab couldn't appreciate her guidance and wisdom until it was too late. What he'd give for one more chat with her, one more time running to her for comfort after losing to Sanu in double siege, or running to tell him about Qala, even though Jab didn't have a crush on her.

He wondered if Hunter was left alone to deal with his abandonment. Whether he was a victim of parental neglect or over attention didn't excuse his actions.

Jab looked at the horizon and estimated how far inland they'd come. It seemed like low hills ringed the mountain in the distance, and the other side of the island didn't have that rocky ring, which must've been where he and Brouglas washed ashore. Where Jandi would've washed ashore too, if he had been a stronger swimmer or not wearing armor.

Too many people around Jab had died. His parents were only the beginning. And Ridgerd would descend on Qawar, Nasalid would retaliate, and the cycle of death would spiral into greater madness. He had to stop it, but there wasn't much he could do while chained.

After they walked for what felt like hours, the sun began to dip below the horizon, a blessed break.

The riders dismounted and shoved Brouglas and Jab onto a log.

Hunter hopped off the horse he'd been riding. "I'll get firewood for us tonight," he offered.

The gopher leader pointed at the cart full of stolen lumber. "We've got plenty of garbage wood. Mulchers don't throw away the unusable bits, so that's what we use for campfires."

Jab wondered if that was the origin of the twigs men wrapped into their beards, but decided now wasn't the time to ask, not that these riders would know, or even care.

Within minutes, firewood was brought over by one of the riders who'd stayed quiet. "Make the fire," the gopher barked.

"Us?" Brouglas lifted his wrists and shook them, letting the manacles jingle together. "Release us then."

"Fine. Be cold." He hoisted the wood back up and brought it to where the riders had seated themselves. One turned his back to the others and stared at Brouglas and Jab, arms folded. "I'm watching you. You'll shiver, but you won't die. It doesn't get cold enough on Coppergrass." His voice came out like a rasp, as if Jab were an idiot for existing.

As the stars blinked to life against the darkening sky and Jab's hindpaws throbbed, he wondered why the All-Planter had done this. If this was a divine test, he couldn't understand why. He was chained here while everyone at home was doomed to die.

"You sleep, lad," Brouglas whispered. "I'll make sure they don't hurt us." He switched languages and lowered his voice. "Don't say you are with Nasalid. They might kill you."

He wanted to protest and retort that Hunter wouldn't let them kill them, but he didn't know if Hunter would have the courage to defy his mother's soldiers if the moment came, or if the riders would even listen. Jab had to listen to Brouglas to survive. He had to find Sanu again.

18

SANU

- Excerpt from Nasalid the Liberator's message to the Frenglese kings.

The carriage holding Yagub, Nett, Sapling Galdwin, and Lady Marjitay disappeared behind a hill within minutes of their pursuit. Despite being in good shape for a kid his age, Sanu was slowing Ridgerd down.

"Keep going without me," Sanu wheezed between breaths.

The hamster slowed his pace so Sanu could catch up. "Never," the king said. "Look to your left and see how your perseverance inspires my banner carriers and trumpeter." Ridgerd turned his head and shouted, "He's ten, and faster than you lot! I must not be drilling you hard enough."

"I'm twelve," Sanu corrected, but the din of their thudding footsteps drowned him out.

"Lungry," Ridgerd pointed at the taller of his two banner carriers. "Return to the ships and tell them there's been a double cross."

"Now, my liege?" the beaver asked between breaths.

"Yes, and tell them if I have not returned by tomorrow's sunset, then disembark and turn the island upside-down until you find me or my corpse. Tell them not to listen to any seedlings who say it's the All-Planter cursing me. We've had enough of that already."

"Understood," Lungry replied, then he turned and ran the other way.

The porcupine trumpeter strained to match their pace. "If that mansion is far, we'll never catch them."

Ridgerd increased his speed, pulling ahead of Sanu, the porcupine, and the last banner carrier within three strides. He didn't even seem tired. "Run as if walking would start a war. Run as if stopping would mean bloodshed. And if what I hear is true, Korpin, run as if your last girlfriend is chasing you."

The banner carrier and trumpeter laughed and found it within themselves to push forward. Sanu did too. He'd outrun all these stupid adults. He couldn't explain why, but he needed Ridgerd to know he wasn't just some kid. His lungs burned, but he pushed forward. At the end of the lane, a mansion came into view, and at the top flew the same banner they'd seen when arriving at Newhouse City: the bighorn sheep with horns fashioned into crossbows.

It reminded him far too much of Lady Marjitay's honking goose and the weapons she used on ZelZaytun's last Sapling. Sanu had hoped she'd get some justice for what she'd done, but it seemed not.

The mansion sported the regional architecture, but the Ganan's Rakes decorating the domes seemed new, as if they'd only been recently added.

At the foot of the mansion, an iron gate in a stone wall rose and quickly shut again as the carriage passed through.

"They'll open it again for a king," Ridgerd said, still showing no signs of being winded.

They were playing double siege again, with the general piece going out forward, and the vanguard rushing ahead, all while protecting the civilians. Sanu hoped there'd be no need for siege engines to get into this mansion.

They rushed down the hill, following Ridgerd.

When the mansion loomed at the end of the long road, the scrape of metal from the alleyway beside them made Sanu's ears perk.

Ridgerd called for a halt, and Sanu skidded to a stop with the breathless banner carrier and trumpeter.

"What is it, my king?" Korpin asked, using his trumpet as a support.

"I think I'm going to puke," the banner carrier moaned.

Sanu straightened and tried to stop breathing so hard. The metal scrape came again. Louder, this time.

"Who goes there?" Ridgerd bellowed. The cramped alleyways around them were cast in long shadows from the buildings' roofs.

Racka-click

Sanu's ear twitched. The last time he heard that was—

Racka-click

"Crossbow!" Sanu checked the rooftops and found a mole rat cranking a large crossbow and aiming it at them from a wooden balcony.

Ridgerd gasped. "Find cover!"

The four of them darted into an alley as a crossbow bolt flew toward them. The point slammed into the road, kicking up dust and loose gravel.

Someone had tried to assassinate the king!

Sanu's heart raced as the shadows protected them. He shoved his back against the building along with the trumpeter and the banner carrier.

Grim-faced, Ridgerd turned toward the porcupine. "Korpin, take my sword. You're the better fighter. Protect them with your life." He handed the sword and scabbard to the slack-jawed porcupine.

"M-my liege, you can't be serious. You need a sword."

The hamster king snatched Korpin's trumpet. "Words are stronger than swords. Instruments play the words of the music world, do they not?"

"What? You're thinking of singing."

Sanu's eyes widened. "You're going to fight someone who has a crossbow with a trumpet?"

Another crossbow bolt sailed into the alley, and Ridgerd ducked, letting the bolt sail over his head.

"Let me go with you," the banner carrier said.

"You won't throw your life away for me," Ridgerd replied. Wielding the long trumpet like a spear, he charged into the alley.

Sanu spied the assassin again, who took position in a second-floor window. "We have to help him."

Korpin shook his head. "We *are* helping him. We need to be ready for his next instruction."

"No way." Sanu had lost his parents already. Jab was lost somewhere, and Ridgerd was the only rodent with the resources to find him and enough appreciation for Sanu to make it happen. And a king didn't deserve to die in an alley like this. "Korpin, does it hurt to lose a quill?"

"What?" The porcupine arched an eyebrow. "N-no, why?"

Breathing deep, Sanu plucked a quill from Korpin's back. "None of us have as strong of a spear arm as the king. Let's give him some weapons."

"He told us to stay here!" the banner carrier whined.

"He's not my king," Sanu said, charging into the open street.

Ahead of him, Ridgerd sprinted into the alleyway, lunging for the discarded bolts.

Racka-click

"He's loading another shot!" Sanu called as he ran forward.

With more agility than a man his size should've had, Ridgerd ducked low to the ground and kicked the first bolt up into his free paw. Rising again, he placed the crossbow bolt in the open end of the tube.

Sanu caught up to him, running awkwardly with Korpin's quill in his paws, dodging left as a crossbow bolt from the attacker in the window sailed toward him.

"Fetch that for me, brave one." Ridgerd brought the trumpet to his lips. With a deep inhale, he pointed the trumpet upward toward the attacker and blew, making a muffled *thoonk* noise.

The bolt arced in the air, more like an arrow from a bow than a crossbow bolt, and it bounced off the window ledge.

"Pellets!" the king roared. He hoisted the trumpet like a javelin.

"Wait," Sanu said, catching up to him, quill in paw. "Use this."

The hamster king's furious grimace shifted to a smirk. "Clever." He snatched it from Sanu and loaded it into the trumpet as their attacker readied another shot. "Tell the others to storm inside that house. We'll have some answers yet."

Racka-click

Phoom!

Two projectiles passed each other midair. A porcupine quill, shot from a trumpet, lodged itself in the mole rat attacker's shoulder. At the same moment, a crossbow bolt raced toward Ridgerd, who rolled out of the way.

"Hit the dirt!" Ridgerd shouted.

The bolt sailed past the massive hamster, directly for Sanu.

He blinked, and a blast of pain ripped through his head, his ears rang so loud the world became muffled around him, and he could not open his eyes.

19

JAB

Yes, stories abound of rodents angering the All-Planter. But is there anything wrong with those being useful myths? The All-Planter is perfect. All-powerful. If that is the case, there is nothing you or I as flawed, fallible, fallen rodents could do to change anything about the All-Planter. Don't you see, that would be like saying we have a degree of power over the Almighty? You must hear how ridiculous that sounds. The good news? There is nothing we could ever do that would cause the All-Planter to stop loving us. Take the stories as guidance, not literal fact.

- Raticenna's collected sermons

Jab opened his eyes to a starry sky.

"Rise, lad," the gentle beaver whispered. He was squatting a tail's length away. "Those brutes and the traitor boy are gnawing logs over there. I'm surprised their snores aren't waking each other up."

Jab rubbed the sleep from his eyes. "Is it morning?"

"No," Brouglas sighed. "But I need some sleep. You keep lookout. You watch one sleep, count to ten, adjust your eyes to watch the surroundings to your left, count to ten, adjust to watch another sleep, and do the same thing with the right side. Keep that pattern. I don't know another way to pay attention to the camp and ourselves since we can only trust each other."

"I understand," Jab whispered.

"I'm sorry to make you do this," Brouglas said as he lay on the grass. "But if they attack us, I need to be able to protect you. Your training was from the best Qawar has to offer but that won't mean much if you're overpowered, and they're all adults with armor and weapons, not to mention they took our new scimitars."

Jab picked at the manacles on his wrist. "I'll wake you if there's trouble."

"And if there is none, let me wake with the sun."

Jab rose and inspected the chain links, examining each one for any sign of weakness. He wasn't about to let Brouglas get himself killed. Though some part of Jab was disappointed that their defeat of the bandits wasn't enough to earn the beaver's confidence.

After checking the entire chain, a weight sank in his heart. He'd missed the daily prayers today.

He released his grip on the chain, took a long look at each of the sleeping riders and Hunter, checked the surroundings for bears, and cleared a spot to make up for the prayers that he'd missed.

Lost as they were, he had no clue where to orient himself to face the great olive Gnaverwood tree in the Holy City, but his best guess was east, so he faced that way and made the prostrations, wondering the whole time if the All-Planter was furious with him for forgetting the prayers or relieved that he'd remembered. He knew Raticenna wrote that there was nothing imperfect rodents could actually do to upset the perfect Almighty, but still, he didn't want to take any chances.

As he rose from the final prayer, a moonlit shadow loomed over him. It was Hunter.

With ice filling his veins, Jab glared back at the spiny mouse. "What do you want?"

"You're a Grovekeeper," Hunter whispered, his words coming out as half-question, half-statement, but it didn't sound like an accusation.

"Yeah, you caught me," Jab said. "But I have nothing to hide."

After nearly getting killed by a deranged Sprouter back in ZelZaytun and then the literal ocean, he wasn't hiding anymore. Scouts were supposed to use disguises and make false backstories on the spot, but Jab was done.

"Um, I'm sorry," Hunter stammered. "I didn't know my mom was going to send everyone away. I would've told her not to."

"What do you mean?" Jab asked.

Hunter gazed at the darkening moon. "That's not why you're here?"

"I washed ashore," Jab said. "I didn't choose to come to this stupid island." The anger inside him rose, along with a twinge of guilt for saying something so cruel. His parents raised him better and the All-Planter expected more. Any place made by the All-Planter couldn't possibly be stupid.

"So you don't know?" Hunter hugged his elbow.

Jab wasn't about to threaten anyone else with a scimitar today. "Come on. After what you did to us, I deserve to hear the truth."

"She... she banned the Grovekeepers from the island. They were put on a boat and sent back to Qawar. Some Mulchers who refused to work for her were kicked out too."

Jab peered around Hunter, checking the guards behind him, all of whom were snoring enough to wake the dead. "Where did the Grovekeepers go?"

"Qawar, maybe? Freng? I don't know. Maybe a smaller island nearby?"

Jab sighed. "They could be anywhere in the entire Great Sea. Is this why the rodents of Rado Town were so cold to you?"

Hunter nodded, drawing a small circle in the dirt with the tip of his tail. "She thought it was what the Sprouters wanted, but when she kicked them out, people got mad because a lot of them had friends, and neighbors, and family who were Grovekeepers. Some of the smaller places were left without important members of the community."

Jab wished he knew the Frenglese word for "pathetic," but another wave of guilt rose. "I'm sorry. I don't know what I would've done if my mother had done something awful to innocent rodents."

"What do you mean, would've?"

Jab was sure he'd said every word right. And then it hit him. "I'm an orphan. My mom has been dead for two months."

"Oh," Hunter muttered. "I'm sorry."

The sun poked over the horizon, casting a streak of yellow that cascaded along the ground, illuminating the not-too-distant sea, and stopping at the mountains in the distance behind them.

Jab stepped over his chain and tapped Sir Brouglas with his tail. For the amount of time that had passed, he realized the beaver was barely taking a nap compared to the several hours of sleep he'd given Jab.

Brouglas was a good beaver, and Jab wished he'd had more charitable ideas about Sprouters, even of Hunter and the porcupine who'd nearly killed him back home.

"Hunter," Jab said, "I had issues with my mom too. And there were times I wish I'd had a different dad. I lost them both. I wish I knew them better. I'm sorry your mother put you in this kind of situation." He felt like he said a wrong word or two, but hoped the message came across.

Brouglas stirred, rising slowly so as not to trip over his chains.

Jab tried to meet Hunter's eyes in a way that was stern but not judgmental. "You need to be honest with her. Like her or not, she's the only mom you've got."

Brouglas yawned and patted Jab on the shoulder. "I suppose this means Hunter apologized?"

"I really am sorry. I won't tell them you're Grovekeepers." Hunter hung his head, and Jab wondered if his neck hurt from doing that so much.

Brouglas shook his head and played with the chains to form the Ganan's Rake symbol. "If you thought only a Grovekeeper would protect another Grovekeeper, then I think you need to learn more about our beloved Ganan, Blest be Him."

"Blest be Him," Hunter whispered.

Jab wondered if his reaction was automatic, drilled into him like asking someone "how are you?" without actually meaning it. He raised his wrists toward Hunter. "What are the odds you can get their keys from them?"

Hunter's eyes widened. "I-I—"

"Come on," Brouglas whispered. "Don't think of it as stealing. Our Gardener Himself told us that giving comfort to a prisoner was a way to honor Him."

Hunter chewed on his lip, eyes glued to their manacles. He turned around as the guards stirred and awoke.

"What's this?" the lead rider asked through a yawn. "You three having a meeting without us?" He pulled his end of the chain hard enough to knock Brouglas off balance and send Jab to the forest floor.

"Let's head out, boys. We've got to pay a visit to the baroness."

The chain tightened before Jab could stand back up, dragging him a few inches. Brouglas and Hunter jogged ahead enough to catch Jab and help him stand while keeping pace.

The sun parted from the horizon, illuminating the island, displaying everything except what Jab wanted to see the most. Maybe it shone on his brother, out there searching for him.

20

SANU

Sanu tumbled in darkness, thrashing in the unknown until a cool, wet sensation snapped him awake. His eyes shot open, revealing Korpin crouching above him.

The strange room's furniture gave the impression of a bedroom too nice for a pauper, but unlike the mayoral mansion they were supposed to be at. Sanu glanced down; he was in a bed, and his clothes were folded neatly on a chair in front of a mirror. His entire left ear was covered by reddened bandages.

"Wh-wha—"

"Shh," Korpin soothed, gently pressing Sanu back into a pillow. "The bandit who shot at us was holding the homeowner hostage. Thanks to my quill, your idea, and the king's ... everything, we're safe."

Sanu's head throbbed so much he could barely think. "What about the mansion? Did he get there?"

"He refused to go until you received attention. The bandit is recovering as well. In another room, under Ridgerd's watchful eye."

Sanu's heart sank. He didn't like the idea of a king delaying his plans for someone as unimportant as him.

"He'll want to know you're awake. He's barely slept."

"Slept?" Adrenaline made Sanu shoot up in bed. "How long have I been out?"

"Only the night," Korpin said. "Please, don't rush it. You're injured."

"But what happened?"

"A miracle." King Ridgerd ducked to enter the doorway. "The crossbow bolt punctured your outer ear. It ripped off some skin and cartilage, but you'll heal, lad. While I don't like the idea of turning my trumpeter's body parts into weaponry, I admire your ingenuity."

Sanu's eyes widened. "I'm sorry for disobeying your order to stay put."

"Ha! Like Droughtlands you are." Ridgerd slapped the foot of the bed. "I think you said it best, that I'm not your king. And it's a good thing to defy a bad order. The house's owner has promised to shelter us until you've recovered and are ready to finish our walk to the mayor's mansion."

"We can't stay here," Sanu protested. "Please just leave me if you have to."

"How about this, my friend," Ridgerd said, running a finger along the foot of the bed. "We'll leave when you can leave the room without stumbling. An ear injury will impact your balance more than you'd expect. And this is not time wasted. That mole rat has been imparting some useful information about why my cousin isn't on the throne anymore." Ridgerd made a fist and shook it playfully. "You'd be surprised how a rodent's tongue loosens when there's a threat of loosening his teeth."

Korpin shook his head. "I don't know why you're trusting the words of a bandit."

"I trust his eyes," Ridgerd shot back. "Eyes tell the truth. If you know what you're looking for, of course."

Sanu tried to follow along, but the pain in his ear swelled. It must have shown on his face; Ridgerd shot a scowl at Korpin.

"I'm sorry, my liege," the porcupine said. "But the boy is a Grovekeeper. If I give him an olive chew for the pain, it'll violate his faith." Korpin sighed, then forced some levity into his voice. "Besides, you already sent your banner carrier back to the boats, so I'd have no more backup."

"Somebody had to let them know we survived." the hamster replied. "Sanu, I'll give you some fermented berry juice. I understand it is forbidden for you, but this will dull the pain."

Sanu breathed hard. Back when he'd thought Jab had died, he tried becoming more religious as a way to honor his presumably dead brother. But after doing that for so long, he wanted it for himself. He also heard stories about rodents who started drinking berry juice and ruining their lives. "Like you said, you're not my king. I'd rather push through the pain and grow from it."

Ridgerd folded his arms. "Now there's a soldier. It's a bit goose-headed if you ask me, but any chivalrous knight always puts the All-Planter first. I admire your faith."

"Thank you. You'll admire my brother's even more," he replied.

"I wish I could say the same about my brother," Ridgerd mumbled. "Rest or walk, Sanu. I'll leave you to it. I don't want to let that mole rat out of my sight." The hamster ducked under the doorframe and left.

Korpin chuckled. "Well, you heard it from the royal lips. What'll it be?"

Sanu breathed deep, then pushed the blanket off, sat up straight, and repositioned to the side of the bed. The tight bandages pulled on his skin, and he yearned to take them off and see the damage. Korpin offered a paw, but Sanu pushed it away. "Thanks, but I need to do this myself. I'm going to be tough, like Ridgerd."

Smirking, Korpin backed away, creating space for Sanu.

Sanu placed one hindpaw on the floor, then the other. He slid off the bed and stood. His head hurt, but this wasn't so bad. With a step forward, his knee buckled. Sanu leaned to the left and then his other knee buckled. Leaning right made him stumble, but he caught himself with his tail.

"You can't walk on a tail like that," Korpin warned. "It's not a crutch."

"What if I had a walking stick?" A pained grin formed on Sanu's face. "Or a walking *instrument*?"

"What is it with people wanting to take my trumpet?" Korpin rattled his quills. "While you were unconscious, Ridgerd threatened to use it like a club against that mole rat. I'll fetch it, but you need to rest some more. Take a jaunt around the room without falling, take a nap, and then I can convince the king we're ready to leave."

"Deal," Sanu said. He stumbled in a semicircle around the bed. His head throbbed, and he couldn't believe how much of a role in balance his ear had played. Everything sounded muffled, but he was sure that would go away once they changed the bandages.

He did another semicircle around the bed, drank some water, and as he crawled back under the blanket, he muttered the daily prayer to himself. He'd started doing it as a way to honor Jab, but this had become more important to him over the last few months, even knowing that his brother was alive. Maybe it was because Sanu wanted so desperately for Jab to still be alive that he was able to take his devotion as a Grovekeeper more seriously.

When Sanu awoke, Ridgerd was stooped over him, changing the bandages on his ear.

"Sorry, Sanu," Ridgerd whispered. "I didn't mean to wake you."

A king getting himself dirty and changing someone's bandages? Sanu didn't know why he let things like this surprise him about the hamster. "Where's Korpin?"

"Downstairs, eating with the homeowner." He loosened the last bit of Sanu's bandages and displayed them. "Only a small bit of red. You should be ready for light travel. *No running.* Want to see your battle scar?"

Sanu gazed into the mirror across from the bed. His left ear had a chunk missing from the middle of the edge, as if a hawk had clamped down on his cartilage and ripped out a section. He was horrified and also really pleased with how intimidating it made him look. All the best warriors had chunks missing from their ears or damaged whiskers from fights. Ridgerd didn't seem to have any, but Sanu wondered if the hamster had ever lost a fight to have a scar like that.

"Not too hideous, but sufficient to make you look tough."

Thoughts of Cladh swooning over his scar flooded into his mind, but he had no clue why. He wasn't still thinking about her and definitely didn't want to impress her. Besides, she was something of a pacifist and wouldn't take well to battle scars. Not that Sanu cared.

"But you look tough without scars," Sanu said.

A sad smile creased Ridgerd's muzzle. "Even without scars like yours, I have enough of a problem fighting people who want to kill me that I don't have time to fight off anyone who wants to marry me. Show me how you can walk and then we'll leave."

Once Sanu did, Ridgerd nodded and motioned toward the door.

They left the house, and the homeowner, another mole rat who was much thinner and older than their assailant, thanked Ridgerd for their service and stay. He offered a pouch of acorns while Ridgerd was shoving their attacker out the door.

Korpin waved to politely refuse the acorns, but Ridgerd stopped in his tracks and faced the homeowner. "We'd be honored. This gift shall not be forgotten."

Sanu hobbled out, using the trumpet as an awkward walking stick.

"We don't need acorns, my liege," Korpin said once they were out of earshot.

"We don't, but *he* needed to give us a gift. You saw how the Mulchers were in the tavern. Giving gifts is a custom here. We wouldn't want to insult the man. Besides, Sanu is a growing boy and he could use a snack."

"The bandit could've gotten away," the porcupine mumbled.

"I have a name," the mole rat said. His accent was thick enough that Sanu had to strain to figure out what he said.

"Tell us then," Ridgerd said, "so I can administer proper justice to your mayor."

"No," he hissed.

They continued on the stone street, attracting decent attention, which made Sanu's heart pound. They'd already been attacked once. Now they were slowed down and exposed.

Sanu matched their pace, which bothered him. Galdwin and Lady Marjitay could've done anything in the meantime without the king there.

"Who paid you to attack a king, bandit?" Korpin demanded.

The mole rat scowled, but his face fell. "I didn't know who you were. I wanted to sell his sword. I figured you'd have a lot of money, by the way you were dressed."

Sanu glared at the mole rat, partially for how seeing another member of Lady Marjitay's species made him feel. And then a realization struck. They were almost at the mayor's mansion, and the Honking Goose herself could have paid an assassin. But that also seemed foolish, since Ridgerd was their best chance at conquering ZelZaytun.

If this attacker had been successful, the invasion may have ground to a halt. So many of these soldiers had personal loyalty to Ridgerd, and Sanu understood why. He would've made that heroic defense and provided tender bedside care for anyone under his command and protection. He'd met other people who were called nobles, but Ridgerd was the only one who seemed deserving of the title.

He just wondered what it was that made the hamster so convinced he would go to the Droughtlands when he died, and why his father was disappointed in him. Maybe it had something to do with him not having a wife, which Sanu thought was a pretty dumb reason to be mad at someone.

They neared the mayor's mansion and the gate in front of it.

Ridgerd shoved the mole rat by the shoulder and addressed the gate guards. "Special delivery for the mayor's justice. Attempted robbery and murder. Tell your mayor that King Ridgerd is here. Send my apologies for not arriving yesterday, but this one here slowed us down. Remind your mayor that I still have not received an official answer for my cousin's whereabouts."

The mole rat grimaced, staring at his hindpaws.

The guard, a spiny mouse, nodded grimly. "Lady Gavrer has been expecting you. She'll be glad to see you. We will take this criminal."

"No," Ridgerd said. "He stays where I can see him until he receives his justice from the mayor. She deserves to know what's happening on her streets. Besides," Ridgerd pointed at his back with his downturned thumb. "Look at this fancy crossbow I got from him. He deserves to watch me carry it around. Perhaps it'll be a gift for your mayor. Gatter, you said her name was?"

"Gavrer," the guard corrected. He tapped the gate three times with his spear, and the metal gate rose into the stone arch above it. They proceeded through a passage that had what looked like a ceiling with missing stones.

Sanu's heart raced. Those were murder holes. Defenders could pour boiling oil or throw rocks down them in a siege.

"What kind of mayor has murder holes?" Ridgerd asked.

"There have been improvements lately." The guard sounded frustrated. "*Upgrades.*"

The group continued under the incomplete ceiling and reached a double-door entrance, which two attendants opened.

The interior reminded him of the Gananhall back in ZelZaytun, but stripped of religious symbols. This long building had a raised platform at the end, with two sets of staircases rising on the sides, and extra rooms branching off the main hall. In the back sat three thrones, a large one coated in gold, and two beside it. To Sanu's horror, Lady Marjitay sat on the left, and the Sapling Galdwin on the right. Between them was a spiny mouse, a female teenager.

"It's good to see you," Lady Marjitay hissed. "We were so worried."

Sanu scanned the room, hoping for a sign of Yagub or Nett, but only stares from a myriad of rodents greeted him back.

The spiny mouse in the center stood. "Welcome, King Ridgerd. You stand in the house of Lady Gavrer, daughter to Baroness Bohbrat. Who have you brought with you?"

"First, my trumpeter," Ridgerd said, indicating the porcupine. "And here we have Sanu, my ward, a brave young squirrel and a fine double siege player." Then the king's voice darkened. "But I also bring before you a common bandit who attacked us in the middle of the day. How are you running this city if someone like this could attack someone like me. How'd he even get access to a crossbow?"

Galdwin stiffened. "My king, that's no way to speak to a mayor."

Lady Marjitay shushed him. "There are criminals attacking nobles here?" She wheeled on Gavrer. "Answer the king's question!"

The spiny mouse's shoulders slackened and she stared at the floor. "I didn't know it was that bad. Mother said the crime would stop when we put everyone in their place."

"Where are the town guards?" Ridgerd asked. "I saw your entourage and some in the mansion, but nobody patrolled the city. Where is the rest of your law enforcement? Did they go when my cousin lost the throne?"

"Your cousin has been replaced by Baroness Bohbrat." Lady Marjitay folded her arms over her chest. "Most city guards were sent to her mother's castle. A private army."

Sanu didn't think this island was big enough that anyone would need a full military. Depriving a city of its guard felt irresponsible.

The king's paw hovered over his sword. "Lady Gavrer, speak it plain. Where is my cousin?"

Gavrer's eyes widened, and a tremor rocked her voice. "M-my mom exiled her to Freng. She said with Nasalid in control of Qawar, Coppergrass needed a stronger leader for when he inevitably invaded."

Ridgerd's exhale came out like steam. "And your mother also deposed the mayor and put you in charge? Know this, I will have words with her." The king shook his head. "Lady Gavrer, I've come to you for another reason. As I hope Sapling Galdwin and Lady Marjitay informed you, we had a boat of soldiers shipwreck onto Coppergrass. We would rescue them and get all of our ships repaired. We were denied full access to your harbor. I will leave this criminal with you, retrieve my soldiers, and be on our way. We do not wish to trouble you here on Coppergrass."

Lady Marjitay whispered something to Gavrer, and she glared at the king.

Steel in her eyes, Gavrer shot back, "No, you already brought trouble. These two told me the truth about you. You're a depraved rodent. You don't belong on Coppergrass. Those soldiers who washed ashore will serve at the capital. They'll join my mother's army."

Ridgerd let go of the mole rat attacker and scoffed. "Ha! Surely you jest. Galdwin, who else will lead the army to the holy island? Do you imagine someone else willing to lead the charge to retake Olihort?"

Hearing ZelZaytun's wrong name stung Sanu, but not as much as the accusations about Ridgerd being cursed.

The Sapling rose from his throne. "Your sins are too powerful to be overlooked, my king. We have already sent word about your death back to the ships. When you didn't arrive last night, we feared the worst. It is out of your paws now."

Ridgerd's nostrils flared, and Sanu's arm hairs raised.

"*I* will lead the troops," Lady Marjitay said. "Olihort's throne is mine, anyway."

"Lady Gavrer, whatever they told you about me cannot be true," Ridgerd said through clenched teeth.

Sanu's mouth dried. He hadn't felt so powerless since watching Jab disappear into the waves. Sanu preferred it when the mole rat almost killed them with a crossbow to whatever this situation was. He remembered speaking out of turn at ZelZaytun, and how much trouble that had brought, and he knew he shouldn't say anything. He wished Jab were here with him. He'd know how to keep calm.

But Jab wasn't here.

"Wait!" Sanu exclaimed. When all eyes centered on him, he fidgeted, almost making him fall over his trumpet-cane. "That Sapling guy also said that Ridgerd could make up for his sins by taking over the Holy City. If—"

But it was too late. Armed guards with pikes advanced on them.

"King Ridgerd," Lady Marjitay announced, "You're under arrest."

21

JAB

- Divine Poetics

Marching across Coppergrass dimmed the sense of beauty it might have had otherwise. Jab lacked the enthusiasm to appreciate the thin bushes that might've been trees or the squat trees that might've been thin bushes. All he had was enough energy to stare at Brouglas's back and paddle-tail, matching his speed to avoid bumping him. Jab owed him that much. If

Brouglas hadn't risked his life to save Jab's, he wouldn't be here. But then Hunter would still be running Rado Town, so at least those rodents had benefited from Jab washing ashore.

Hunter kept staring at the ground. Jab wanted to ask if that bothered his neck, but anytime he spoke, one of the riders gave them a hard time.

"How much longer until we see the baroness's castle?" Brouglas asked.

The lead rider spat from atop his horse, nearly hitting Jab's hindpaw. "When you quit complaining."

Even if Jab hadn't been getting better at understanding Frenglese, the gopher's tone would've told him everything.

Hunter piped up. "They deserve to know. They didn't do anything wrong."

"Yesterday you said they kidnapped you," the rider grunted. "So which is it?"

"I, uh." Hunter hugged himself and stared at the horse's hooves. "I think you should tell them when we'll get to the castle. I would if I knew."

"It's your own castle, you worthless sop," the gopher said. "You never got around to learning about this island?"

Brouglas wiggled the chains. "He would've spent his time learning to speak proper. Watch your language. You're wearing the symbol of our Lord Ganan's Rake, Blest be Him. Show some respect."

Jab tensed. There would be a consequence for that, but Jab didn't mind. He remembered being around Grovekeepers who weren't representing their faith well, and he wished he'd had the courage to speak to them then as Brouglas had to this brute now. Jab regretted so much of what he'd thought of Sprouters growing up. They couldn't all be bad.

The lead rider yanked the chain hard enough to make Jab and Brouglas fall down. "You think you're funny, do you? I'm wearing the baroness's symbol because she pays me to catch vermin like you."

Jab pushed himself up with his tail, springier than Brouglas attempting the same. Jab wished Brouglas had his armor and that they both had weapons. They'd take care of these brutes real fast, or at least wouldn't be pushed around by them.

Jab looked over his shoulder, watching the carriage, laden with the stolen wood, roll behind them. He wondered which was more valuable, the lumber or him and Brouglas. Maybe if he could find some way to mess with that carriage and the lumber, that would give them a chance to escape.

But he needed to rid himself and Brouglas of the chains in the process.

As they all pressed forward, Jab kept watch for any jagged rocks that could be used for leverage. He had no way to talk to Brouglas without them overhearing, but he did have a way to communicate in a way that would be meaningless to the others.

Jab could speak Qawari. There'd be another lashing out, but he accepted it. "Sir Brouglas, how can we escape these chains?"

"Shut up!" the lead rider shouted.

Brouglas let out a dry chuckle and replied in Qawari. "Ganan, bless for him, says bad loses to itself. Give them minutes."

"Minutes?"

"Um... time."

"Shut up, I said!" The brute yanked again on the chain, which made his horse huff and skitter sideways.

Hunter looked up at the noise. "Stop it," he whispered.

"If his horse bolts, we'll be stuck along with it," Jab said.

"What part of 'shut up' are you too stupid to understand?" The gopher called for a halt. He dismounted, and the other riders stopped, angling their horses toward Jab and Brouglas.

Brouglas eyed Jab. "Your tail... how strong? Grab key?"

Jab stretched his tail at the question. "Maybe, but—"

The lead rider pulled out a short sword from its place on the saddle, displaying the blunt end and still holding the chains with his other paw. "How about I knock you both senseless and drag your bodies to the baroness?"

Advancing, the brute brandished his weapon and Jab's heart raced. He couldn't grab the keys off him with his tail, and even if he could, the other riders were all right there.

Brouglas stiffened and changed languages. "You'll be sent to the Droughtlands if you attack the boy. I don't care what the baroness is paying you, nothing will outlast eternity. You might get forgiveness for killing me, but you know what Ganan said about harming children, Blest be Him."

The lead rider scowled. "You'll wish for the Droughtlands when I'm done with you."

"Go on, then," Brouglas taunted. "Show your brutes how to attack a knight whose paws are tied together."

"I'm not challenging you to a fight." He lunged forward, stabbing at Brouglas.

The beaver knight stepped into the blow, catching the blade between his inner arm and his ribs. "Jab, run trip him!"

Grunting, Jab whipped his tail at the leader's ankles, making him fumble the blade and the chains.

Holding the blade between his arm and side, Brouglas stepped back and angled the hilt upward. Brouglas brought his head down, and clenched the sword's pommel between his teeth.

The other riders dismounted. They only had seconds.

Jab let go of the gopher, took the sword from Brouglas's teeth, and placed it in his bound paws.

"That's the spirit, lad." Brouglas said as he adjusted his awkward two-pawed grip. He pointed the sword at the lead rider's neck and called out to the others. "Let us go or explain this to your boss."

As the other brutes gaped at each other, Hunter jumped onto the now-riderless horse their tormentor had used. He snatched the reins and pulled the horse in the opposite direction.

Their one ticket off the island galloped away while Jab and Brouglas were still bound, outnumbered, and completely lost.

22

SANU

If history remembers me as a failure, leave Qawar, change your name, and dye your fur. All I ask is that when people curse me for losing to the Frenglese horde, know in your heart that I did my best, and that I loved you and your mother more than I could ever describe.

- General Ironseed's last letter to his son

Soldiers wielding devilbeaks surrounded Ridgerd and Sanu.

"Surrender, lad," Ridgerd whispered. "We'll fight another day."

Sanu lifted his paws over his head. A burly soldier pulled Sanu away, and he was forced to watch as the others closed in on Ridgerd.

The king turned an eye toward Sanu and winked. Ridgerd lifted his paws in the air, and as the soldiers took another step forward, he slammed his paws down in a clubbing strike, knocking two devilbeaks down. The other two soldiers gasped and stabbed. With a grunt, Ridgerd rotated, getting the weapon stuck in his crossbow and out of the attacker's paws. He twirled, and the other soldiers retreated a step.

Sanu felt his captor's grip loosen. He'd only have one chance at this. Despite the throbbing in his head, one thing was clear.

He was done letting things happen to him. He would take charge.

Sanu ducked out of his captor's grip and pulled out the knife attached to his hip, almost stumbling in the attempt. Though he lacked the tail grip strength to pull a weapon out of an adult's paws, he could climb. He lunged up the mole rat's back and reached for his helmet, twisting it to the side and obstructing his vision.

The guard snarled and dropped the devil-beak as he righted himself. Sanu made a quick cut on the guard's belt, letting his pants fall to his ankles. He rolled away and grabbed his trum-pet-cane while the royal hamster kept spinning, keeping the other soldiers at a distance.

"Catch!" Sanu shouted, hoisting the instru-ment and letting it sail in the air. He wished he was strong enough to fight alongside the king.

King Ridgerd snatched the horn and adjusted his grip, wielding it like a club. He bashed a sol-dier's face with the wide end, letting him fall to the floor. Sidestepping another devilbeak stab, he pulled back for another strike, this time to the attacker behind him.

Ridgerd's clothes were in tatters and he was bleeding, but he'd fended off the soldiers.

"As for me being under arrest," he said between heavy breaths, "I disagree. You don't have many other guards here, do you? Your mother took all the good ones to the capital with her."

The assassin mole rat who they'd brought with them scampered away in the fracas. Sanu cursed at the idea of someone like that getting away.

Lady Marjitay and Sapling Galdwin had disappeared as well. The prospect of the two of them being missing along with the mole rat who'd attacked them twisted a knot in Sanu's stomach.

Sanu stepped over a guard who was massaging a bruise where the king had horn-smacked him. He debated cutting more belts, but he knew a bunch of defeated rodents when he saw them.

"Is this what you truly wish for?" Ridgerd asked. "To imprison a king?"

Gavrer hung her head. "I... I'm sorry. They told me you were cursed and that I was keeping everyone safe by arresting you. I thought we could send you back to the Freng islands and that your ransom would impress my mother."

"If that is the type of thing that would impress her, I'm sorry to say she might not be the kind of rodent worth impressing. Now, there were two other younger rodents who came over with the two who deserted you. Where are they? Those two can speak to the lies about me being cursed."

"The squirrel guy and the porcupine girl?" Gavrer asked, all confidence bleeding from her voice. "They're in the basement. The Sapling said they were criminals."

Even after his time among Sprouters, Sanu didn't completely understand the difference between a seedling and a sapling. The extent to which these rodents followed the bad ones was shocking. If Galdwin had been like the noble one in the Holy City, he would've understood, but Gavrer must've just met Galdwin today.

"They aren't criminals," Sanu said. "I bet he told you that because they would've said King Ridgerd didn't do whatever bad things they told you he did." As many times as Ridgerd had brought it up, Sanu wondered what the seedlings back on the boats were saying about the king, and how many rumors they were allowing to blossom in his absence.

"I can tell you this much, young Gavrer," Ridgerd said, returning the horn to Sanu. "Your mother is not the rightful ruler of this island. She called an army to herself and placed her child in power because she feared local retaliation. Just rulers don't worry about that."

Sanu wondered then why Galdwin and Marjitay had it out for Ridgerd. Maybe they were just jealous of what a good leader he was. No other explanation came to mind.

"I thought my mom would take care of the problem of the poor in Copperfort." Gavrer retreated to her throne and slumped in it. "I thought everyone liked her."

The king knelt and helped an injured guard stand. "Tell your mayor the truth of it."

The guard, a jerboa who looked like he could've had ancestors on Qawar, thanked the king and spoke to Gavrer. "When your mother banned the Grovekeepers, whole neighborhoods had to readjust. The extra tax on the Mulchers is not having a good effect. Crime has been increasing."

"Why didn't you tell me?" Gavrer asked, eyes wide.

"We are just guards, not advisers."

Ridgerd helped another guard stand, and Sanu did the same, offering the trumpet for leverage. He winced knowing it was the same trumpet that had knocked a molar loose on this guard.

"Lady Gavrer, would you have listened to your guards?" Ridgerd asked. "Would you have done things differently if you had another chance?"

"Of course," Gavrer replied. She straightened and addressed the squirrel guard. "Karayat, fetch the two that the Sapling and noble tricked me into locking up. King Ridgerd, what should I do?"

The hamster nodded slowly. "I have some ideas. First, you will tell me where my shipwrecked sailors are and where my cousin, the rightful ruler of Coppergrass is. Second, you will allow the soldiers on my docked ships to disembark. Third, you will listen to your guards and workers henceforward. They have greater insight into matters than you might believe. Turn a compassionate ear and a generous paw toward the poor, and the rodents will love you. Do you agree?"

"The shipwrecked sailors would be at my mother's castle by now, and that's really all I know. My mom said the old queen was cursed and needed to be ousted. Nobody told me why though." Gavrer left the throne and ran toward Ridgerd. "I accept your terms. I'll start right now."

"I have one more condition." Ridgerd's voice darkened. "Point me in the direction of your mother's keep. I feel that is where the Sapling and Lady Marjitay have fled to. I'll have words with all of them about my cousin. If you don't honor your side of the bargain, I have someone in mind to replace you and enough siege equipment to render this mansion to rubble."

23

JAB

I've told you before about my father's friends, a Mulcher and a Sprouter, men so dear that I called them uncles. A student chastised me once for this. We worship the same All-Planter, despite disagreeing on specifics. Of course I believe Grovekeeping is the truest way to the All-Planter, and part of that is loving my neighbors. I'd call a good Sprouter a neighbor before I'd say the same about a miserly Grovekeeper.

- Raticenna's collected sermons

The sword clutched in Brouglas's paws trembled. Without Hunter, Jab and Brouglas were truly lost. Even if the beaver knight could defeat these other riders with a significant handicap, they had no idea where they were. Any path could lead them back to Rado Town as surely as it could lead them to the awful baroness everyone kept blabbing about.

The riders closed in on Brouglas and Jab.

"How about a truce?" Brouglas asked. "I could end your leader's life or you could let us go."

"We can't go back to the baroness empty-pawed," one of the riders snarled. "Especially with a smaller crew."

Jab peered at the riders galloping away in the distance after Hunter, which drew his gaze to the carriage with the wood they'd pilfered from the Mulchers. Jab tried to think of ways he could get that carriage to turn around. If he could get that away from them, they really would have to turn back. But that might get him and Brouglas killed.

"You have the wood," Jab said, impressed with his increasing ability to speak in Frenglese. "Take that back. Tell your baroness your other friends got lost and your other horses did too."

The other riders pressed in, and Brouglas leaned forward, pushing the sword blade against their leader's throat. "Do as the boy says. You don't want your leader's death on your paws."

A dark red circle was spreading on Brouglas's shirt, starting by his ribs where he'd caught the sword. They couldn't do this much longer. He needed medical attention.

"Brouglas is famous in Freng. Valuable beaver to you. Let us ride in your chariot." Jab hoped he'd used the right word for "carriage."

"Just do it," the gopher hissed.

"Not good enough," Sir Brouglas replied, breathing heavier. "You'll tell your baroness that we are not your prisoners. That we are emissaries. He from Nasalid the Liberator and me from King Ridgerd. We were shipwrecked here. International law demands she speed our travel."

Jab wasn't sure what "international law" meant, but he assumed he'd misunderstood. If different kingdoms could agree to international laws, why would conflicts happen in the first place?

"Deal," one rider said. "Back off the gopher and we'll take you to her. But we're keeping your swords. Get in the carriage."

Sir Brouglas backed away slowly, and the chain's tug pulled Jab back as well. He hated the idea of staying with these brutes, but he wasn't about to let Brouglas go much longer without a healer. He wished he knew more than the basic stuff he'd learned as a scout for Nasalid, but whatever cut the beaver knight had suffered was too deep for a simple stitch.

Jab's heart raced at the possibility of an infection or bleeding to death, two ways to die that Jab couldn't stop.

Jab climbed into the carriage first and helped Brouglas sit beside him, which required both hands and his tail. Brouglas dropped the sword at his feet, and the lead rider heaved off the copper-tinted grass, dusting himself. The others helped him stand, and placed him on the carriage, with his back to the driver.

Driven by hunger, Jab asked, "How long until we reach your baroness?"

The lead rider glared at Jab. "One day."

That night, Sir Brouglas groaned through a fitful sleep, but Jab stayed wide-eyed, ready to give his protector the meager bit of water he had, and keeping a lookout for the brutes. Nobody had returned with Hunter and the remaining riders murmured to each other in a way that made Jab's skin crawl. He needed Brouglas. This beaver was his savior. He wasn't about to let him die.

Jab used his scout knowledge to apply as much healing as he could. He knew to change bandages and to keep the wound as dry as possible, but he didn't know the early warning signs of an infection, only that he needed to cut around the fur that was matted down with the blood. He wished Kash or Maimon were here—the scout and the physician. They would've known what to do.

He tried to channel them, his teacher and surrogate older brother, and the Mulcher philosopher who taught Jab to be more open-minded. Maimon had tended Jab's own wounds. He'd distracted Jab with questions about faith and Jab hadn't noticed the procedures he did at all. Maybe that was the trick. When Brouglas woke, Jab would keep the beaver's mind off the pain. Maybe that was all he could do without supplies or compassionate escorts.

But the way these riders discussed the baroness, he wasn't sure how much help they'd receive in the castle. They had to have a healer there. They just had to. Brouglas deserved better than this.

When he was convinced the riders were all sound asleep, he rummaged through the wood. He knew some fungi that grew on trees could be applied for medicinal effects, but as he searched the timber, a thought struck him. If he didn't know precisely what kind of mushroom he was looking at, he could just as easily poison Brouglas.

It wasn't worth the risk. The only mushroom he'd found growing on one of the stolen trees crumpled to dust the second he touched it, anyway. He wished he knew more about the local trees. What he'd give to read a book, even one about things he didn't particularly have an interest in.

Brouglas's breathing grew heavy, and Jab did the one thing he knew he wouldn't get wrong. He found a leaf that had stuck to a tree trunk, and he used it as a cloth to wipe the beaver's brow. It wasn't much, but it was the best he could do.

The first glimmers of sunlight peeked over the horizon. The morning had come too soon. He had stayed up all night and there was a new day coming. He'd feed Brouglas his breakfast if nothing else, assuming they survived the night.

Traveling across the island in a carriage full of stolen lumber grated on Jab more than walking. Brouglas's breathing steadied, and his bandages didn't need to be changed nearly as often, but Jab couldn't shake the feeling that Brouglas's injury went beyond the flesh. He wondered if metal could poison a body somehow. The swords here probably had a higher copper content, but Jab didn't know enough about metals to understand what that could've done to Brouglas. Kash and Maimon would've known that too.

The golden sun made the grass shimmer a brilliant yellow-brown, as if the grass forgot it was supposed to be green. If he wasn't sitting beside an injured beaver, it would've looked beautiful.

They crested a hill, and a rumbling noise shocked him. It started as a low murmur, but grew as they climbed the hill. At the peak, Jab found the source. An army was drilling in a field below, in the stretch of land leading to a dark castle.

Among the banners, he found two designs. The first, he didn't recognize: a bighorn sheep with horns fashioned into crossbows. While the design was shocking, it was in the minority among the soldiers. He couldn't count more than five, and he realized those were along the sides, across the field, as if they had been there before and were announcing arrivals to the castle. The other, more numerous flags he saw were ones he had seen before.

Those were flags from Frenglese princes.

These were soldiers in front of a foreign castle, and they were not attacking it. They were drilling, which Jab learned in his time with Nasalid.

These soldiers were practicing for combat.

24

SANU

When my nephews quarreled, I reminded them that despite their differences or who was wrong, they were still brothers. I would hate for a similar speech from the All-Planter to the two of us on Pruning Day. I will write to the Five Princes. We'll get a better trade rate to Freng. Anything to stop this bloodshed.

- General Ironseed's letter to the Frenglese general

Exiting the throne room gave Sanu a different feeling than entering it. Gavrer was sobbing. *Was leaving her in power right?*

Maybe she'd learned her lesson. Sanu remembered his own mother. He would've done anything to make her happy and he would've given anything to have her and Dad back alive. Being with Ridgerd didn't bring his parents back, but it did dull the pain of their absence.

The apologetic guard led them to the cellars, where Yagub and Nett were chained to support beams. The guard walked with a limp from where Ridgerd had clubbed him in the knee with a trumpet. "S-sorry we attacked you, m'lord."

"You were following orders, my friend," the king replied. "Valiantly so."

Yagub and Nett glanced up as the trio descended the stairs.

"Don't tell me you surrendered," Nett said. "Wait, you're not chained?"

Sanu hobbled down the steps, afraid to lose his balance with his damaged ear.

"What happened to you?" Sanu's gaze sharpened to a glare. "What did they do to you?"

"All is well," Ridgerd said at the bottom of the steps. He had to duck to fit. "We had a misunderstanding upstairs, courtesy of Marjitay and Galdwin's lies. We're here to release you and be on our way."

Nett pushed off the support beam to stand. "Just like that?"

"We nearly got impaled by devilbeaks," Sanu muttered. "Marjitay and Galdwin escaped."

Yagub shook his head. "They told everyone in the castle about you, my king. Everything, I'm afraid."

"What do you mean, 'everything'?" Ridgerd demanded.

The guard shuffled over to Nett and undid her chains.

She rubbed her wrist where the chain had been. "They told them everything they needed to make a loser fear and hate you." It seemed like she wanted to say more, but after looking at Sanu, she kept quiet.

As the guard moved to undo Yagub's lock, he hastily nodded without making eye contact.

The hamster king sighed. "I was wondering how long it would be before they spewed poison."

Sanu pounded his trumpet-cane into the cellar floor. "Can't you just say they lied about whatever it was?"

Ridgerd frowned. "Good liars tell partial truths. If I deny their claims with words and not actions, I won't be believed. I bet if I had a wife, they'd shut their cheese-holes."

"You're a good hamster, my liege," Yagub said as he stepped away from his chains. "Perhaps we can find you one. A suitable queen who would silence any rumors about you."

With a worried look at Sanu, Ridgerd shook his head. "Let's be off. We have some business to attend to. And you two, no more getting into carriages with corrupt nobles."

As they started up the stairs, Nett har-rumphed. "I seem to remember being ordered into that carriage."

They left the mansion and followed Ridgerd through the city, retracing their steps.

After an hour of walking, Ridgerd, Korpin, Yagub, Nett, and Sanu passed the spot where they'd been attacked. Seeing the chipped stone from the crossbow bolt sent a chill up Sanu's spine and made his damaged ear tingle.

He never wished to return to this place.

By the time they neared the docks, Sanu's hindpaws throbbed, but he became confident enough with his balance to return the trumpet to Korpin.

"We're stopping here," Ridgerd announced.

Yagub raised an eyebrow. "Why here? Did you want more of that loov?"

Sanu realized they'd stopped at the tavern from the day before where Ridgerd had trounced him in a game of double siege. "Shouldn't we go to the ships?"

"We have business here. Come on." Ridgerd led the way, and Nett scurried to his side. With a bowed head, he opened the door and let her enter first, then Yagub, and Sanu last. Closing the door behind Sanu, Ridgerd leaned over to whisper. "You have a good ear for assassins. Keep an eye out for us."

Sanu nodded, glad his hearing wasn't damaged.

At the king's entry, the owner let out a joyful yelp and hobbled over, his twig-tangled beard swinging as he walked. "What a great surprise this is!"

Because they weren't close to a meal time, the place was empty, except for a single beaver and squirrel near the counter with big mugs of berry juice. Sanu's heart raced at the prospect of it being Jab and Brouglas, but the squirrel was a bit too old and the beaver's shoulders too narrow for it to be his brother, not to mention Jab was too devout to ever drink berry juice. The prospect of leaving this island without his brother stung, but he still didn't know where to look or whom to ask.

By the time Sanu realized his mind had wandered, Ridgerd and the owner were deep in conversation.

"You honor me, King Ridgerd," the red squirrel said, "but how could I perform such a task?"

The king straightened. "A leader looks after his own, manages money, and treats everyone with respect. I know little of Newhouse City and its woes. You will be part of the solution." His voice softened. "My cook still needs your recipes though."

"Then I accept," the owner said, bowing.

"Korpin, remain here and make sure no trouble stirs. Listen for where my cousin was sent in exile, or if her actual fate was death." Ridgerd dismissed the porcupine and addressed the others. "We have some news to deliver to those on the ship," Ridgerd said, holding the door. "This city shall come under royal protection until we sort out our business on this island."

25

JAB

Hear, O rodents! Different languages and customs among the Great Sea's islands are not meant to be points of division. Experience new ways of thinking. Learn from each other.

- Divine Poetics

Jab stared slack-jawed at the army before him. These were troops pledged to King Ridgerd for his invasion of Qawar. Too few to be the full force, but at least a full ship's worth of soldiers. Maybe the ship that went off-course hadn't been taken by the wind.

"By Ganan's Rake," Brouglas muttered.

The riders exchanged glances with each other, whispering to themselves.

"Can you hear what they're saying?" Jab whispered.

"Not really, but I can tell they're surprised."

The carriage and riders approached the field where the Frenglese soldiers drilled. The lead rider grudgingly removed Jab and Brouglas's chains, and Jab stretched his aching wrists. Brouglas slumped forward, wincing.

When they were close enough for Jab to notice the individual soldiers' species, one near the front spotted them and called out. An armored squirrel on horseback rode up to their group. His metal armor had an unusual wear pattern, as if something had been removed from it. By the shape on the knight's chestplate and an uneven wear pattern, Jab guessed this knight had removed a symbol or coat of arms.

The knight stared down the riders. "Halt. What business do you have in the hall of Baroness Bohbrat?"

The lead bandit snarled and limped toward him, his own black armor a stunning contrast to the squirrel knight's. "We work for her. Who in the Droughtlands are you?"

Wincing and supporting his injured side, Brouglas eased off the side of the carriage. "Hail, sir knight. I am Sir Brouglas, part of King Ridgerd's army. We were separated from everyone else."

The knight maneuvered his horse, getting a better look at the beaver. He pushed up his helmet's visor, revealing himself to be a squirrel. "Consider yourself fortunate. We were cursed by Ridgerd's sins. We should never have followed him."

Jab arched an eyebrow. He only had a few interactions with the king, but he'd seemed to be a decent hamster with the exception of wanting to invade Qawar.

Sir Brouglas puffed out his chest and groaned like he regretted it, nursing his wound. "Doesn't Ganan, Blest be Him, tell us that we have all sinned and fallen short of the All-Planter's glory?" He slipped into a coughing fit on the last word.

Jab stepped up beside Brouglas. "He needs medicine. He is hurt."

"Your accent," the squirrel knight mused, "are you Qawari?"

Not a good question. "Yes, but can we please get Brouglas inside the castle? He is hurt."

The lead rider stomped his hindpaw. "I need answers. Who are you and why are you talking like you have any authority here?"

Every hair on Jab's neck stood at attention. This wasn't good.

The knight dismounted and pawed the reins to Jab. "If you can ride, get him inside. I'll help you hoist him." As Jab complied, Brouglas followed him up, pulling on Jab's tail as a counterweight.

Turning his attention to the lead rider, the knight injected some ice into his voice. "I'm the highest ranking noble among these soldiers, and they're now my responsibility. The seedling aboard appointed me the leader, and I have accepted Baroness Bohbrat's offer to stay on Coppergrass Isle and defend her from all threats. It seems you have some wood to deliver. Deliveries are taken in the back." He helped his horse turn around, then walked beside Jab and Brouglas, navigating through the stream of armored soldiers.

Jab's throat tightened as they neared the castle, which cast a heavy shadow over the yellow-brown grass. It loomed over them, the largest building he'd seen since washing ashore. It blended the architectural styles of the fortresses he'd seen in ZelZaytun and in the map books Nasalid had with the Frenglese style he'd seen when they met King Ridgerd the first time. Stone towers rose from the sides of the main building like spears or a chair turned upside-down.

A crown pattern formed near the top, which could provide cover for archers raining down death from above. The castle's walls butted up to the cliffside overlooking the Great Sea. He wondered how many soldiers could fit inside as a garrison and if this was the only castle on the island, a central capital ready to defend and destroy any passing ships.

The magnificently horrifying building made Jab wonder how Nasalid's siege engines would fare against it and how Nasalid was faring on Qawar. He hoped at least somebody was enjoying the peace.

When they reached the wrought iron gate, he wondered if the army's presence here might mean King Ridgerd's invasion of Qawar would stop altogether or at least be weakened. Maybe it was a good thing that they were here. With the exception of some bandits, this island seemed peaceful.

But then he remembered the lumber and the oppressed Mulchers. If half of what Hunter had said was true, then this island was not in a good place under Hunter's mother. The knight escorting them explained that Brouglas was injured and a fellow knight, and the gate rose with a *racka-click*, as if it were a gigantic crossbow.

As the gate opened, the squirrel knight turned to Brouglas. "How did you get injured?"

"Self-defense," Brouglas muttered.

Jab eyed him, wondering why the beaver hadn't revealed that the baroness's goons were to blame.

They passed under the castle wall's entryway, the ceiling webbed with iron. Standing on the iron supports, an archer glared at them. Jab wondered what other nightmares they could rain down from that vantage point. Burning oil seemed likely, and the thought made his skin crawl.

Closer to the castle's main keep, Jab noticed arrow slits rising up the building. This castle was built to withstand attacks and repel invaders. He wondered if an invader would even bother upon seeing this place.

How could they get enough food here? How many other oppressed Coppergrass Mulchers toiled to support whatever huge garrison must be here?

The knight took them inside a set of double doors, and helped Jab and Brouglas off his horse. The castle's interior was expansive, an atrium meant to impress and bamboozle. Art and tapestries covered so much of the wall that Jab forgot he was in a stone building. The knight directed them to follow him as servants and workers milled around . Jab wondered why nobody had come to greet them, but with Brouglas's heavy breathing, he'd fare better without a welcoming committee.

They looped through a hallway and down a spiraling staircase. The passage led to another door, and the knight rapped against it. The armored gauntlet made a *thunk* against the door and a grumble came from the other side.

"I have a wounded knight here," the knight said. "A Frenglese beaver. Allow us entry."

The door groaned open. A hunched-over mole rat stood on the other side. "The baroness didn't tell me anyone was coming. Your seedling will find out you're bossing us around and won't like it."

The squirrel knight glowered at him. "Didn't you take an oath to heal the wounded?" He motioned for Jab to enter, helping Brouglas limp beside him.

The mole rat harrumphed and motioned to a chair.

Jab marveled at the rows of shelves in this cramped space, full of bottled mushrooms and a rainbow of liquids.

The knight helped Brouglas get situated, but the mole rat kept his agitated grimace.

"The baroness will want to see him if he's really another noble," the healer said, pulling a bottle with a creamy red liquid off a shelf. He uncorked it and sprinkled in some dust from a dried mushroom.

Lacking a healer's delicate touch, he yanked off the beaver's bandages, earning a wince.

"Hey! He's a..." Jab realized he didn't know the Frenglese word for "veteran." "He's a fight soldier." Veterans deserved respect; Jab knew that would translate into any language. And as he felt his defensive instinct rise for Sir Brouglas, he realized a painful truth. Brouglas may have killed Grovekeepers, some of Nasalid's soldiers, rodents Jab may have spoken to or eaten with, during the siege of ZelZaytun when they were on opposite sides.

And this knight who'd brought them inside ultimately wanted to put more Grovekeepers to the sword.

Yet this awful healer was hurting someone he was supposed to help. Jab wasn't sure who was his enemy anymore.

Jab felt like he barely knew who *he* was, anymore.

Brouglas waved a paw. "Don't worry, lad, I'd rather finish this sooner." He spoke with his eyes closed tight, as if each word was agony.

The mole rat rubbed the creamy solution onto Brouglas's wound.

Brouglas writhed like a worm stuck under a rock. "Ha-haa-haa... that's hot."

"It burns the wicked spirits that enter and make infections. It'll dull your pain while I work."

The mole rat grunted at the knight, making him step back out of the way. The healer dug through his supplies until he found a needle and thread. Jab wished he had been able to stitch Brouglas up himself when he'd had the chance, but the important thing was that they had survived to get here.

"When will they be ready to meet the baroness?" the knight asked. "I agree that she'll want to see them. Boy," he turned his attention to Jab. "Do you have more information about that snake, Ridgerd? We know what the seedling told us, who got his information from the Sapling himself. Some of the troops remain unconvinced of the king's sins, but if you had more to share, that might convince them. Is there anything you saw or heard that could persuade them?"

Brouglas winced as the mole rat began stitching him. "Don't say anything, lad," Brouglas said. "Sir knight, don't speak such things around the boy."

Jab's stomach convulsed. He hadn't been this unsettled since the siege of ZelZaytun when he'd been attacked by a traitor and nearly killed. If part of Ridgerd's army splintered off, he'd be protecting Qawar. The first time Jab had lied, it tore out his heart. Since joining Nasalid the Liberator, he felt like he'd become less holy as he helped in the liberation of the Holy City, which seemed backward. And even now on Coppergrass, he'd barely prayed, and when he had, it only brought him trouble. He'd told his lies in the service of being a spy. Protecting his life and others.

Maybe he could do that here.

"I will tell you about Ridgerd," Jab said. "But I am still learning Frenglese. Who here speaks Qawari?"

"The baroness has a translator and a merchant who speak it," the knight said. "She'll want to see you immediately."

Brouglas sighed, and the pain on his face wasn't from the stitches.

Disappointing him hurt more than his own willingness to lie.

26

SANU

I heard you refused to accept a Sprouter recruit. Our enemies are not all Sprouters everywhere. The invaders happen to be Sprouters. All true sons of Qawar deserve to fight for our freedom. You denied us a sword arm and may have delivered one to our enemy, one who knows our land well.

- General Ironseed's reprimand
to a failed sergeant

Sanu's hindpaws felt unsteady as he returned to Ridgerd's flagship, but the worried and relieved expressions on the sailors' faces showed him that waiting had been just as harrowing for them.

"King Ridgerd!" the captain exclaimed, running over. "We feared the worst and were ready to descend on the city until your banner carrier arrived. Gossip flies around the ships. Sending messengers on rowboat between them these last two days has been taxing. Preventing bored seedlings from spreading confusion has been a chore. Keeping the siege engine parts clean and ready for deployment has been our main distraction."

"I can imagine," the king replied. "There's not enough room in the harbor for all our ships, but we'll disembark everyone. Two ships at a time will unload their soldiers. One detachment will keep watch over Newhouse City, and the others will come with me."

The ship's squeaky wood under their hindpaws bobbed in the gentle waves.

Sanu's tail stiffened. Keeping watch over the city sounded more like an occupation. Ridgerd had his own replacement ready to depose Gavrer at a moment's notice.

"Where are we going, my lord?" the captain asked.

"There's a castle where a cruel rodent rules. I have reason to believe our lost compatriots are there. I won't continue to Qawar without them. This will be a simple rescue." The hamster tensed and his tone darkened. "Or this will be a fine chance for our soldiers to test their blades before we descend on the holy island."

Sanu's heart plummeted to his stomach like a stone. He didn't know what the peaceful solution was, but he needed to find it as much as he needed to find Jab. Maybe all the washed-up rodents ended up at that castle and Jab would be there. Sanu turned around, facing Newhouse City, the one he swore was named ZelNuhas.

He didn't know if Ridgerd's soldiers would be a welcoming and calm presence or seen as hostile invaders.

But there was nothing he could do. Swept in the wave of kings and baronesses, Sanu felt as adrift as his brother.

As the captain prepared messengers to send the news to the other ships, Ridgerd turned to Nett.

"You are one of the only seedlings in the force I know is loyal to me," the hamster said.

Nett folded her arms. "My loyalty is to Ganan, Blest be Him. It so happens that you are also a king I find noble, and I've seen how deceitful Galdwin can be."

"True, but I need you to communicate with the other seedlings," Ridgerd said. "Explain what transpired with Galdwin and Marjitay. Their deeds should be public, and I find it harder to believe her innocence involving Olihort's last Sapling. We cannot bring them to the holy island with us. Catastrophe and deceit follow them."

"I'll help," Yagub piped up.

"Of course you will," Sanu mumbled.

"Her word carries enough authority, Yagub," Ridgerd said. "She doesn't need an escort."

Nett's paws fell to her sides. "He can come with me if he likes. Besides, you need him away from the front lines since you need a translator and guide on Qawar."

The hamster scratched his chin and turned his gaze toward Sanu. "I think I would extend that to you, as well, my young friend. You need to heal and your services on Qawar will be invaluable."

Sanu straightened. "No. I'm coming with you. If you're crossing this island, I'm joining you. My brother is out there, and I won't find him visiting a bunch of seedlings in your army."

Ridgerd let out a laugh that shook Sanu's whiskers. "Ha! I suppose if I command you to stay put, you'll say I'm not your king. Accompany me, but you won't be my shadow when it comes time to draw swords. You've been injured once on my watch, and I won't have your death on my paws."

"Thanks." Sanu wasn't sure how he felt about Ridgerd planning for more fighting.

Hours later, the ships were still unloading. They would've been on the move much earlier, but Ridgerd dragged out the ships' disembarking. The whole day, he'd stood at the docks and greeted each individual soldier as they left the gangplank.

Sanu nibbled on a small version of the loov. It was good, but it was no sheltercake. Sanu wiped his mouth, rubbed the crumbs off his paws into his shirt, and began the sunset prayer.

Sanu completed his prayer, finding solace in knowing that if Jab were on dry land, he was making that same prayer somewhere too. Sanu sat on the dock's edge, letting his hindpaws and tail dangle over the calm water.

Ridgerd slapped each soldier on the back, thanking them for their patience and loyalty. He asked each one their name and reminded them they were pilgrim soldiers on the way to the holy island, here to save their lost brothers-in-arms. Sanu wondered how much was the hamster's personality and how much was politics. The idea of a nasty rumor about the king itched at Sanu's mind, especially not knowing what it was or why nobody would say it in front of him.

As Ridgerd greeted each soldier, their faces showed how much their spirits were brightened by the king's attention, even if they'd only had a few seconds of his time individually.

The night dragged on, and Sanu lost his battle with his eyelids.

He awoke the next morning in the Mulcher's tavern with Yagub at his bedside. "Hey, there's the brave warrior."

Sanu sat upright in the bed he didn't remember entering, rubbing sleep from his eyes. A faint aroma of loov tugged at his nose. "What's that mean?"

"Korpin told everyone about how you saved the king's life. You helped the king beat an assassin."

"It wasn't really like that," Sanu said. "That's an exaggeration."

Yagub gently undid Sanu's bandage and pressed some ointment into his ear. "Your missing ear chunk here says otherwise. It looks like somebody took a bite out of it. It makes you look tough."

Cool. Sanu pushed the covers off and moved to the edge of the bed. "Are we about to leave?"

Yagub nodded. "The king asked the seedlings to have one big Offering Meal service for all the soldiers and invite the Sprouters in town to join us. They don't have a Gananhall here, so there's no Sapling to preside, but the local seedlings are going to be there."

Pretending he understood all of that, Sanu got out of bed and examined his ear in the mirror. It would take time to fully heal, but he did have a sense of balance again. "Is that where Nett is?"

"Yeah. She's not leading the service, but she'll be there. King Ridgerd said he wanted someone else to lead the service so it wouldn't look like favoritism. Which is bad, I think, because the seedling with the most seniority is one of Galdwin's lackeys. Who knows what foul things he'll utter about Ridgerd?"

"But what are those bad things?" Sanu pressed him.

Yagub sighed and joined him at the mirror. "I don't know how to tell you. Or even what to tell you. It's the kind of thing that could ruin some-one's reputation. If he'd just get married, the whole thing would be put to rest."

Sanu scratched his head. "If I could find him a wife, do you think he'd call off the invasion?"

Yagub raised an eyebrow. "I don't know if anything will get him to do that. I don't want another war in Qawar, but you, your brother, and Sir Brouglas are the only people who think like me as far as I can tell. We've got to do our best to arrange for a summit between Nasalid and Ridgerd. If you could find someone he'd marry, he'd definitely be less plagued by rumors and gossip."

Sanu nodded. The only adult women he knew were miles away in Rattin, and Lady Marjitay. But getting Ridgerd to meet a woman from Rattin would still require getting the king over there. Playing royal matchmaker wasn't his dream in life, but if it got the religious leaders off his back, then maybe the pressure to invade would end. If finding Ridgerd a wife could stop a war, Sanu would do it.

He could not let Ridgerd set hindpaw in Qawar.

27

JAB

As a rule, I try not to laugh in people's faces. Yet a youngster once told me he's not afraid of Pruning Day because he's never done anything wrong. He'd do well to meet a taciturn Sprouter; they will be the first to tell you that pride is the sin which makes for the surest route to the Droughtlands. The good news for him is that he has time for age to humble him.

- Raticenna's collected sermons

Jab's resolve to stay by Brouglas's side strengthened as the beaver's breathing returned to normal. He'd survive, thanks to the healer's medicine.

Brouglas slapped the stone floor with his tail. "What medicine did you give me?" he asked the healer. "Ganan, Blest be Him, insisted we never use witchcraft."

"'Witchcraft,'" the healer snorted. "The All-Planter provides. That was olive oil mixed with berries and mushrooms."

Jab's mouth dried at the mention of olive oil. That they had it meant it was imported from Qawar, which could only come from the sacred Gnaverwood. For them to take those olives and eat them was one thing, but to make oil out of them for medicine didn't sit well. It felt like invading the All-Planter's space.

And telling lies about King Ridgerd to stop a war might be too.

"Ah, that's no surprise then," Brouglas said. "It makes food taste better and it can revive wounded skin."

The knight had remained quiet, perched against the wall, propping himself with one hindpaw. He pushed off the wall and came between them. "Ready to meet the baroness?"

Brouglas cast a warning glance at Jab and nodded.

When they left the cellar and started up the stairs, Brouglas whispered to Jab in Qawari. "The king is a good rodent. Please, no lies."

"I'd tell them anything to stop a war," Jab said. "Can you think of another way to stop this invasion?" The All-Planter warned them about spreading falsehoods, but the Divine Poetics also insisted rodents work for peace. What if a lie was the only way to get it?

"Stop muttering," the knight said. "You sound suspicious."

"I'm sorry," Jab replied, switching languages. "Freng is not my first language. I don't want to say the wrong thing in front of the baroness."

They reached the top of the stairs. The grand hall remained unchanged, with servants and guards crisscrossing in the upper and ground levels, carrying weapons and food. The hectic energy unnerved Jab. He remembered the bustle of Nasalid's camp, when too many soldiers and servants were pushed together in too small a space.

This baroness was preparing for an attack.

They marched up a purple carpet on the grand staircase. Copper lined all the railings and fixtures along the inside. After climbing the second set of steps, Brouglas was winded again.

Nothing good ever seemed to come from lies, but preventing war and death might be the exception.

The prospect of what he was preparing to do weighed on him more with each step, but he pushed it off as nerves before meeting the baroness, hoping she was nothing like Lady Marjitay.

Two mole rat guards blocked the door, wielding devilbeaks. Upon seeing the knight, they nodded and opened the double doors.

Inside, copper laced the stonework floor, as if molten metal fused the stone together. Light through tall stained-glass windows mixed with the copper, giving the room a gold-tinted rainbow glow.

The purple carpet rolled all the way to the back of this grand throne room, leading to a spiny mouse upon the throne, a woman with dark fur and sharp features, seated under a long tapestry detailing a coat of arms: a bighorn sheep with crossbow horns.

A trumpeter stood by her side. Upon Jab and Brouglas's entry, the trumpeter blew a *gwah-gwah-goooh* and placed his horn by his side, which was long enough that it could've been a walking stick. Jab internally chuckled at how silly that would be, but his thought was interrupted by the trumpeter's booming voice. "Defectors from the cursed Ridgerd, you stand before baroness Bohbrat, protector of Coppergrass and savior of the Sprouters."

Savior? Jab had been called the savior of his hometown by Nasalid, and the title embarrassed and confused him. He hated the pressure and attention that single word put on him, yet this baroness had made it part of her title.

The squirrel knight who'd been escorting them placed his helmet in the crook of his arm and bent at the knee to salute her. "My lady, I have Sir Brouglas, a hero from the Battle of Phranktonbourg, and defector of Ridgerd. With him is an emissary of Nasalid."

Baroness Bohbrat nodded slowly and narrowed her gaze on Jab. "The boy is an emissary?"

"Yes," the knight replied. "I think Nasalid sent a boy emissary as an insult to the late King Hedgry, and Ridgerd was unable to understand."

Jab hoped he'd misunderstood the squirrel's words.

"My cousin fought at Phranktonbourg." The spiny mouse shifted her attention to Brouglas.

"And how is it that you did not arrive on the ship with the other defectors?"

Brouglas bowed his head. "I don't think I know your cousin, but I'm sure he was a great warrior. I washed ashore with young Jab."

Jab's cheeks flushed. "I fell overboard on Ridgerd's ship. Sir Brouglas risked his life to dive into the ocean and save me. That's how we ended up here." The baroness's sharp features made her appear both beautiful and stern, commanding, but not like Gizlee.

"Your ship was not guided off-course by the same miraculous wind that brought the others to me?"

The knight shook his head. "They do have information about the cursed king though."

"You do?" Bohbrat asked, leaning forward. "That would prove quite useful in getting the rest of the soldiers to swear loyalty to me."

They were calling King Ridgerd cursed. Agreeing felt wrong. Disagreeing might lead to innocent rodents dying. Sometimes when he closed his eyes, he saw the flames of battle again. At night, the crunch of bones echoed in his sleep. He didn't want that for anyone else.

Jab breathed deep. "Ridgerd is cursed because war follows him. ZelZaytun is in Nasalid's paws now. Ridgerd will bring unnecessary war to Qawar. Nasalid promised protection for all Sprouters who want to visit the Holy City as pilgrims. There's no need to fight over it."

"ZelZaytun?" Baroness Bohbrat repeated the word with irritation. "You're a Grovekeeper?"

"Y-yes, I—" Jab stammered.

"Wait, no!" Brouglas lunged forward.
"Arrest him!"

28

SANU

Fog rolled over the yellow-brown grass outside Newhouse City.

Sanu earned a place of honor astride a horse, with Korpin marching alongside the banner carrier who'd joined them on their way to meet Gavrer. Ridgerd marched on hindpaw, refusing a horse to match his rodents-at-arms.

Leaving Newhouse, the army marched wide enough that Sanu could only just see the edges of the troops by squinting left or right.

"It's impressive, isn't it?" Korpin asked.

"I don't know." Sanu had dreamed of joining an army, yet those dreams were reserved for fighting for Nasalid against the Frenglese colonists who'd invaded Qawar. Marching in an army with rodents who could've been the invaders' grandchildren made Sanu's stomach plummet.

"Uneasy before battle?" Ridgerd glanced over his shoulder and Sanu felt ashamed knowing the hamster heard him. "Don't worry, it won't come to that. I've heard tales of Nasalid's generosity, and I scarce believe the lies spewed by Lady Marjitay."

Sanu wanted to ask why bother invading at all, but his embarrassment kept him silent.

Ridgerd arched an eyebrow. "You don't believe me?"

"I do," Sanu admitted, "I just don't see how that will work. Your soldiers think they're pilgrims."

Ridgerd shrugged. "Some are in it for the coin. Others the adventure. I know Korpin is running from his ex-girlfriend."

The porcupine chuckled. "You know me well, my liege."

"But Sanu," Ridgerd continued, "You've seen me fight. I cannot lose. You'll speak to Nasalid. Yagub as well. He'll know victory against me is impossible and leave Olihort without any bloodshed."

Sanu's whiskers stiffened. "He said any Sprouters were welcome to make pilgrimages there. You don't have to show up at all."

Korpin fidgeted in the saddle. "Careful," he whispered.

Sanu braced for the hamster king to shout at him.

Instead, Ridgerd sighed. "I doubt Sapling Galdwin's honesty, but not his authority. He says I'm condemned to the Droughtlands. He and half the seedlings I've ever met have told me that the only way I can earn my way out is by fighting my father's enemies. Father's final wish was to bolster Olihort's defenses, so I must liberate it after avenging my deposed cousin here. Isn't it curious none of the Saplings agreed to stop calling me a sinner if I focused on helping the poor instead of fighting?"

Sanu shifted like his tail had turned into goo, unable to meet the king's eyes.

Ridgerd gestured to the troops. "The soldiers are truly here as pilgrims, trying to rid themselves of their misdeeds too. They believe their only way into the Walled Garden is by making themselves warriors of Ganan, Blest be Him. Do you want to take that from them, Sanu? Do you want to prevent them from the good afterlife?"

Sanu hung his head. Even his plan of finding Ridgerd a wife felt like a dead end. He had no recourse. His only option was to trust the king and the All-Planter.

The thick fog dissipated, showing they'd started uphill. This road was said to go to the capital, the castle where the baroness reigned.

If Sanu couldn't stop a war, maybe he could at least plead his case to her and she would help him find Jab.

Everything seemed wrong.

They traversed the island over the next day, passing farms and wide fields of short grass.

When the army camped for the night, Ridgerd demanded his chef bathe before making Sanu's meal, so any olive-based ingredients would be off his paws when he prepared the food. Sanu found the order both kind and humiliating. He felt eyes on him when he prayed. He decided when the army was having their morning prayer service, he'd offer all of his daily prayers at once in that span.

When morning came, the soldiers left their tents and flocked toward the camp's center where they had their Offering Meal. Sanu found it a strange name for a community prayer service, but he appreciated the moment of personal silence.

He snuck away from the camp, both lonely and relieved to be alone, and climbed a nearby hill. His ear didn't sting anymore, but feeling a breeze where skin and cartilage used to be was a new experience.

On the hilltop, the morning mist didn't feel as cloudy, and the farms in the distance had shrunk to dots, little mills where they pressed olives. He didn't know much about how plants worked, but he knew olives came from the great

Gnaverwood back on Qawar, and this metallic island didn't have its own Gnaverwood tree, only the squat things that were practically bushes. He wondered if the Sprouters had taken olives from Qawar and tried planting them here, only to fail and produce cheap imitations. He supposed that was better than taking them from the holy island.

A distant pattering caught Sanu's attention. It came from the other direction, and it sounded like a gentle rain, but seemed to come from the ground. Squinting through the morning fog, he found vague ovals taking shape. His eyes widened. These were rodents on horseback, possibly enemies, bandits, or innocent traders. Sanu planted a hindpaw to run to the prayer service and warn them, but these oncoming riders might know something about Jab.

A dark thought surfaced.

If these were enemies and they attacked, maybe they'd do enough damage to convince everyone pressuring Ridgerd to back off.

The band of riders came through the fog, and he noticed they weren't wearing armor. After a deep inhale, Sanu ran toward them.

Sanu prayed that the All-Planter would keep him safe. He was doing this for Jab and for Qawar.

As they approached, the profile of these riders became clear. At the front was a spiny mouse, a teenager who was maybe Gavrer's age, a hamster near Ridgerd's age, and a grizzled mole rat with a crossbow hitched to his saddle. The spiny mouse was dressed in fineries, and the other two like commoners.

Behind those three, a troop of rodents dressed like farmers and blacksmiths followed, some carrying pitchforks and fishing spears. A few others had crossbows attached to their saddles.

When Sanu realized these rodents had more weapons than he was comfortable with, it was too late.

The hamster at the front noticed him and called for a halt. Sanu realized the word she'd used was Qawari, but her accent didn't sound familiar. It was almost like the eloquent version of when Brouglas tried to speak Qawari.

The other riders strutted to a stop, and the woman called out to Sanu. "Jab? Is that you?" Her words came out in a mix of Qawari and Frenglese, and it took Sanu a moment to process what she'd said.

"You know Jab?" he asked.

The woman's eyes widened, and she nodded toward the mole rat before turning her attention back on Sanu. "I'm Gizlee of Rado Town. We're trying to rescue your brother. He told us he had a twin."

29

JAB

- Divine Poetics

A devilbeak was weaponized cruelty. Pointed like a spear, with a hammer and pickax point on the sides. Puncture, crush, shatter.

Two devilbeak spearpoints pressed into Jab's back, forcing him from the baroness's throne room, despite Sir Brouglas's shouted protests. Jab was grateful, knowing the beaver knight tried to save his life again. Not even three months ago, Jab never would've imagined so much kindness from a Frenglese Sprouter.

That same cruelty now shoved him out, allowing one last look at the throne room's long ceiling-to-floor tapestry.

The two guards poked and prodded Jab through the castle interior, toward the steps he'd taken with the squirrel knight to the cellar, but this was oriented in a different direction, and allowed him to appreciate another ceiling-to-floor tapestry in the grand foyer. This banner was even longer, trailing from the top floor to the bottom.

As they approached the main level, large double doors swung open, revealing a small troop of soldiers accompanying two rodents he hadn't seen since the shipwreck. He would've given anything to see Sanu or even Jandi, but it was Lady Marjitay and that Sapling, Galdwin.

His heart sank as he locked eyes with them, knowing they weren't here with anyone who would help him.

Why they'd come without King Ridgerd gnawed at Jab, but the weapon at his back didn't let his attention linger for too long. At their prodding, he plodded down a winding staircase, going underground and into a dank chamber.

A long row of iron-barred cells greeted him along with the stench of mold and decay. A low chorus of moans issued from the cells, and Jab would've preferred ghosts to the reality. Bone-thin rodent heads peeked out of the cages, grasping the bars with paws blackened by dirt and despair.

The guards shoved Jab to the ground, causing him to collide with the stone. While he lay on his stomach, a guard placed a metal clamp around Jab's wrist, linked to a chain, then the guards hoisted him up and pushed him into an open cell. Breathing deep and refusing to scream or cry, Jab glanced down at his wrist. They had chained him to the bars of his cage.

He moved to the left, to a stone wall separating him from the next cell. He didn't need his tail to touch the right side.

In the opposite cage, an old jerboa sat cross-legged, staring back, drawing circles in the dust with his whip of a tail.

The guards who'd shoved Jab gave him one last scowl, then marched out without a word. A heavy wood door slammed shut.

Tears welling in his eyes, Jab slumped to the floor. He'd held out hope that Sanu had been searching for him this entire time. But nobody would find him here.

His parents were dead. And in this cell, he'd found something worse than death. The low moans pulsing through the hallway were those of other prisoners.

"Serenity to your family," a ragged voice said.

Jab wiped his eyes and looked up. He hadn't heard that greeting since leaving Qawar. It was what Grovekeepers said to each other. "T-tranquility to your home." Jab almost forgot the response.

The ragged voice belonged to the jerboa from across the hall. "You look Qawari. Do you tend the All-Planter's grove?"

Another tear came to the surface, and Jab nodded slowly.

"I wish I could offer some sheltercake." A weak wiggle waved through his whiskers. "But I'm out of cinnamon."

Jab's tail stiffened. "How did you know?"

"Brown squirrels don't live on Coppergrass unless their parents are from Qawar, and you wouldn't be down here if you were a Sprouter." The jerboa huffed and came up to his cage's edge. "But what I must know is how you evaded the cleaning out."

"Cleaning out?" Jab asked. Some of the other prisoners had come up to their bars, peering in Jab's direction.

"How long have you been on Coppergrass?"

Jab furrowed his brow. He struggled to count the days. It felt like a lifetime. "A week, I think. I fell overboard a boat and washed ashore."

The jerboa folded his arms over his chest, and the chain attached to his wrist let out a rusty jingle. "Were you coming to save us? Are you with the Liberator?"

"What?" Jab asked. "Nasalid is in Qawar."

"Bah." The jerboa's smile soured. "We'd heard he defeated the Honking Goose. Soon after, the wealthy Sprouter families conspired to overthrow our queen. They claimed the Grovekeepers and Mulchers were plotting to expel all the Sprouters from Coppergrass."

"Nonsense," another prisoner scoffed. From the side, Jab couldn't tell the speaker's species, but he heard the same despair from the moans.

"So the Grovekeepers are in prison?" Jab asked.

The jerboa shrugged. "We were given a chance to become Sprouters. We refused. See what good that did us."

"Stop blaspheming," another prisoner called. "The All-Planter will send us to the Walled Garden."

Jab's grip on his iron bars slipped. Sent to prison for their faith. He couldn't imagine Sir Brouglas doing that, or any of the Sprouters Sanu got close with in his time with them. "Did that many reject the faith? How many of you are down here?"

"We don't know," the jerboa said. "There could be another hundred prisons across the island like this."

Another inmate slammed his bars with his shackles, the metal *clang* echoing down the hallway. "My cousin in Rado Town was sent on a ship to Qawar. His whole neighborhood was."

Someone else groaned. "Not this again."

Jab remembered Rado Town. There had been empty-looking homes near the prayer hall. And then he remembered the Mulchers in that labor camp. "What about the Mulchers?"

The jerboa scowled. "They could cut their beards and become Sprouters or pay a tax."

"The twig tax!" a prisoner grunted. "I'd pay a tax to stay outta here."

Jab remembered the philosopher-doctor who tended to Nasalid, Maimon the Mulcher. He'd taught Jab more about the All-Planter in a few conversations than entire books had. Staring into the old jerboa's eyes, he wondered how much longer they'd be left to rot here.

As despair bubbled in his chest, he remembered Lady Marjitay and Sapling Galdwin's arrival. If they had their way, even prison wouldn't be safe for the Grovekeepers. He needed to do something.

"How often do the guards come?" Jab asked. "We need to escape."

Another inmate smacked his iron bars and let out a sarcastic laugh. "Good idea, kid. None of us thought of that."

The jerboa sighed, which caused his wide ears to sag. "We've tried tunneling out. None of us found a loose stone, and we can't get our shackles or chains to break. Some of us are still trying."

Remembering escaping death from the Sprouter scouts before the ZelZaytun siege, Jab inhaled deep. "I was with Nasalid's spy corps. I met him. He's a good rodent, and he wouldn't want us to be here. I think I know a way out."

30

SANU

Lay down your weapons or risk ruining the neigh-borly balance we've known for centuries. Withdraw, apologize, and return as pilgrims. When my full force musters, we'll be unstoppable.

- General Ironseed's entreaty to the Frenglese general after the siege of Mouse

Knowing Sanu had been right about Jab's survival didn't do much to ease the pain of hearing that Jab was in danger. He didn't know how well he could trust Gizlee or the spiny mouse beside her, but he took them towards King Ridgerd's tent once they agreed to lay down their weapons.

A spear-wielding lookout stopped Sanu and the group in their tracks.

"I found these travelers coming," Sanu explained. "They have information King Ridgerd needs."

Soldiers were filing back to their tents in the distance.

Gizlee urged her horse forward and spoke in perfect Frenglese. "If your king is marching on the baroness's castle, he needs to know what I know. You have no siege weapons that could possibly overtake it."

"How do you know?" the lookout asked, shifting in his leather armor.

"My grandfather designed the walls and keep," she said plainly. "I know its layout and its defenses. There aren't large enough boulders here for your catapults to throw, assuming you brought some. Not to mention I know who inside that castle is still loyal to King Ridgerd's family."

"They laid down their weapons so they could talk to the king," Sanu said. "We can have them talk in the open if you don't trust them."

"I'd prefer that," Gizlee said. "You all should know what I do about the baroness."

"If this gets back to me in a bad way..." The lookout shook his spear.

Sanu sighed and marched the group toward Ridgerd's tent, accompanied by the guard.

The king cranked a crossbow outside his tent. His movements were strong and fast enough that the *racka-click* sound came out more like falling pebbles. He aimed and fired a bolt into a melon that was set in front of a tree. As the soldiers watching him clapped, they noticed Sanu and Gizlee and got the king's attention.

Seeing Ridgerd and Gizlee meet sent a wiggle of shock through Sanu. The two hamsters had a commanding presence, demanding attention and respect.

"K-king Ridgerd," Sanu stuttered, "I present Gizlee of Rado Town. She has information about the castle."

Both hamsters bowed to each other. King Ridgerd set his crossbow in the grass, leaning it against a tentpole. "Gladly met. Your timing is fortuitous. We're about to come to the Copper Citadel."

Gizlee curtsied. "I am sorry about your cousin, good king. I loved her dearly and was with her until the last moment. She was a ... good friend to me."

"Thank you," Ridgerd said. He shifted a fraction, and his tone felt less kingly. "She wrote to me last year, detailing a friend she loved more than life itself. I had a friend like that, but my father sent me to war to drive a wedge between us. It's nice to meet you."

A silence passed between them, and Sanu couldn't understand what kind of conversation they had with their eyes.

Gizlee's ears twitched. "We can discuss that later since we have more pressing matters now."

"Agreed. I'll hear what you know about this castle," Ridgerd replied, voice strengthening.

"I will be honest with you; I have a defector from the baroness with me." Gizlee indicated the spiny mouse teen beside her. "This is the baroness's son."

Sanu felt stupid for not realizing it before. "Is Gavrer your twin?"

The spiny mouse nodded. "I'm Hunter Bohbrat. My mom put us in charge of Rado Town and Newhouse City. I didn't really want to do it, so I got the smaller town. I didn't know what she was doing to the Mulchers or the Grovekeepers. I... I'm sorry."

King Ridgerd tapped the Ganan's Rake symbol on his armor. "I'm a Sprouter, so don't apologize to me. What happened to those groups? Did your mother kill my cousin?"

Hunter stared at his hindpaws. "I thought she'd sent her into exile, but I'm not so sure. She sent the Mulchers from Rado Town to labor camps. I thought she'd given them jobs in the citadel. And the Mulchers disappeared. I *thought* they were sent to Qawar, but..."

"I'm no stranger to being forced into unwelcome positions by my own parents." Ridgerd let out a dry chuckle and pointed at his crown. "You and Gavrer aren't even adults. She set you up to fail. We'll sort this out. Find a peaceful way." He cast an eye at Sanu. "My friend here is a twin too. He's been searching for his brother. I wish I had the bond they have with my own brothers. In your time on this island, have you found another young squirrel like my friend Sanu, here?"

Gizlee stepped forward. "We have. He and a beaver knight saved our town from bandits, deserters from Nasalid's army."

Ridgerd's ears perked up. "That's them!"

Sanu cocked his head. "Was my brother and the beaver knight with another rodent? A squirrel? He was a soldier named Jandi."

"I'm afraid it was just those two," Gizlee lamented. "They mentioned losing another rodent."

Ridgerd let out a grunt that shocked Sanu. He kicked the dirt, sending up a clod of grass. "Pellets! I had hoped that grouchy squirrel sergeant had survived. I don't like the idea of telling Nasalid I don't have one of his trusted messengers when I meet him."

The word "meet" lightened Sanu's spirits some.

Exhaling, Ridgerd fixed his gaze on Gizlee. "What do I need to know about this castle?"

"Your siege weapons won't damage it. The cliffs are too steep for catapults, and the slopes to the entrance are too slippery for battering rams." A hint of mischief snuck into her eyes. "At least, not from this way."

Sanu leaned closer, and so did Ridgerd. Other soldiers had congregated, pressing in on them in a semicircle.

"If you take the long way around, you'll get past the hill and reach the fields. From there, you'll be able to roll a battering ram to the castle, but there won't be ammunition for your catapults."

Two seedlings approached, paws folded and heads bowed. One pulled her hood back, and Sanu was disappointed that it wasn't Nett, but a beaver.

"My king, take her words with caution," the seedling said. "They could be spies."

"A spy?" Gizlee scoffed. "The baroness wishes."

Beside Gizlee, the burly mole rat who had accompanied her harrumphed. He would've looked big beside anyone except King Ridgerd. He sputtered something partially in Frenglese and Qawar, and Sanu tried to make sense of his words. "Baroness took my wife. We are not her friends."

Hunter stepped back from Ridgerd and faced Sanu. "Your brother just wanted to find you. He told me about Nasalid. The beaver knight was brave and tried to protect me. He saw the best in me, they both did, but I got scared. I ran away when we got captured."

Gizlee placed a paw on Hunter's shoulder. "Hunter is making up for what he did to our town. He's honest." She turned to Ridgerd. "Can you feel the truth of our story, good king?"

"I do like 'good king,'" Ridgerd replied. "We shall follow you around this hill. I would lose a day's march to ensure the safety of my soldiers. Take us to the field, and know we shall repay treachery."

Sanu shuddered, remembering the king's brand of "repayment." If this was leading them into a trap, at least he would be by the king's side.

But as skeptical as Sanu was, they couldn't have just correctly guessed Jab's name and that he was Sanu's brother. Enough of their story was true that he needed to believe it, for his own peace of mind, something that would be in short supply once they began the siege.

31

JAB

It's funny, a student of mine wished me luck this morning. "I hope you win the debate," he said. I told him I'd rather "lose" today, since that will mean that I have learned more.

*- Raticenna's debate with a
Mulcher philosopher*

Jab's stomach convulsed. The Droughtlands were sometimes called the "Liar's Realm," because of the Divine Poetics' warnings about dishonesty. Jab hated himself for all the lies he'd told since his parents' death. If a lie could save lives, was that a good thing? Some disguises needed more than just a physical difference.

After explaining his plan to the other inmates, two agreed with his plan, one being the old jerboa. He wondered if it was desperation that convinced them to go along with him. He hoped it was because of his connection to Nasalid, that the very idea of the Liberator was enough to get them motivated.

Three other prisoners said they'd rather die but wouldn't expose them when the time came.

Most prisoners, too many for Jab to count, slumped back in their cells.

After an hour that felt like a month, footsteps thudded from the other side of the heavy oak door to the jail cells. Jab straightened and approached the edge of his cage, wetting the inside of his mouth. He hated how it dried when he lied.

The door swung open and a guard he didn't recognize entered, holding a bucket and a ladle.

The other inmates retrieved small bowls barely bigger than cups and held them out between the cell bars. Jab peered around his cell and found an upside-down bowl in the corner. He wrapped his tail around it and brought it to his paws. The guard plodded down the hall, ladling liquid into the bowls.

When the guard approached his cell, Jab extended his bowl. "I'm ready to take the vows. I want to be a Sprouter." He realized he'd spoken in Qawari and switched languages. "Taking vows I am ready. Sprouter I want to be." He knew he sounded dumb. Being around Brouglas and Gizlee made him more confident in his speech, and something about this place leeched that from him.

The guard stepped back and arched an eyebrow. "So soon?"

"I believe in Ganan." That sentence came out simple, and it was partially true. Ganan was mentioned in the Divine Poetics as a great teacher, just not a Gardener. Mouth drying, he added, "Blest be Him." He'd heard Brouglas say it enough times in both languages that Jab at least knew he wasn't getting that wrong. And it was still partially true, since Jab believed all rodents were blessed by the All-Planter, but whenever the Sprouters said it, the phrase gave Jab a sense of them also saying that nobody else was as blessed as Ganan, which felt wrong.

The guard set down his bucket and ladle and peered at Jab. He spoke slowly. "You reject the Grovekeepers?"

A tear tried to form on Jab's eyelid. He had no other way out of this place. "I do. Time I spent with Sprouter knight. Taught much things."

"Wait here." The guard retrieved his ladle and continued serving the other prisoners, skipping Jab.

When he finished, Jab waved for his attention. "Friend mine," he pointed to the old jerboa, "Speak Frenglese he can't. He will Sprout too."

The guard narrowed his eyes at the jerboa, who nodded. The old timer placed his face against the iron bars and spoke in the mishmash language Gizlee and Yumruk used. Jab tried to understand him, and it sounded like he said hearing Jab describe Sir Brouglas had convinced him, and that he'd been trying to decide for a while now.

The guard plodded out of the room, slamming the oak door behind him.

When his thudding footsteps faded, the jerboa shook his head. "We had to lie and it didn't work. He just left us here."

"They'll just kill us all and be done with it," another prisoner moaned.

"He's probably going to get a seedling," Jab said.

An unseen inmate tutted. "I don't know what you said to him, boy, but the All-Planter did. The All-Planter can see your heart."

Jab pressed his head against the iron bars. "You're right. And the All-Planter can see that I'm doing this to help us get free."

"One lie is like a wheel let loose down a hill," the jerboa said. "But I'd rather take my chances with the All-Planter than take them down here. The All-Planter is at least merciful."

More footsteps echoed, this time two sets. Jab hadn't been here long enough to know when the meals came, but it certainly felt too early for another one.

The thick door creaked open, and the same guard returned, but following him was a middle-aged man, a mole rat with a bent whisker.

The guard plodded over to Jab and the old jerboa. "These two," he said. "These are the ones who will Sprout Anew."

With a wrinkly smile, the seedling reached out to grasp Jab's paw. There was warmth in his grip that should've been in the soup. He used the mishmash language. "Good. This makes me happy. Ganan is good, Blest be Him." Because he spoke slowly, Jab felt like he understood. It wasn't as clear as when Gizlee spoke, but the seedling's slow and honest enthusiasm provided some clarity.

The seedling turned to the old timer and patted his paws in the same way. "This is so wonderful. Two new souls saved by the Gardener's grace. One young and one old. Step away from your cage so the guard might release you."

The guard grunted and the seedling released the jerboa's paws. Turning toward the guard, the seedling pushed his wrists against his hips. "Don't you grunt at me," he said in Frenglese. "They are not able to overpower you. We should be happy they have made the decision. They will be our brothers soon." He leaned toward the guard and his voice became stern. "You would do well to start treating them like they already are."

The guard folded his arms over his chest and glared at the seedling. "Tell them to back away from their cages. I still have protocol to follow."

Jab wasn't exactly sure what "protocol" meant, but he backed to his wall and turned around so his stomach pressed against it. If he had good flexibility, he might've grabbed the keys from the guard's paw with his tail, but he wasn't skilled enough for that. The guard unlatched the door and slipped Jab's chain off the fixture on the floor and into his paws.

"Come on, then," the guard huffed, pulling gently on Jab's chain. Jab turned around, bowed his head like he'd seen Sprouters do, and quietly left his cell.

The seedling gave Jab a gentle hug around the shoulders. "I'm proud of you. You'll know real happiness soon."

"Thanks," Jab said, trying to sound as honest as possible. The guard shoved Jab's chain into the seedling's paw. "You take him upstairs if you're so confident he repented."

"What about the other one?" the seedling asked.

The guard shook his head. "One at a time."

Jab's heart dropped. He'd wanted to save them all and this had seemed like the surest way. He hoped the old timer would be able to get out. All Jab could do was trust that the guard would come back, but he'd still have to verify on his own. This seedling seemed much nicer and accepting than the guard, which made Jab feel even worse about lying to get out of his cage.

The seedling sighed. "We'll come back for him. Let's get you upstairs first. You can sit for our Offering Meal."

Jab followed the seedling up the stairs. The guard plodded behind them at a leisurely pace, muttering something as he walked.

"What is your name, young one?" the seedling asked.

"Jab. I'm from Rattin."

"Rattin?" the mole rat paused and then his eyes widened. "That was the town ransacked by Nasalid, wasn't it? We heard about how he burned it to the ground because he'd trapped Sprouter knights there."

Jab focused on his hindpaws. None of that was true. Jab would know—he'd been there himself. The battle happened outside the city and it was soldiers against soldiers, and no homes were touched. But the flames were very real, especially when they came back in Jab's nightmares.

"Or is there a different Rattin?" the seedling added. "I assume you are from Qawar and that's the only Rattin I've ever heard of."

"I'm from Qawar," Jab said. "But remembering that day of the battle is painful for me."

"Ah," the seedling said, clicking his tongue. "I am sorry to have asked. How did you come to Coppergrass?"

Climbing the spiral stairs was disorienting and much different than coming down. He needed much more focus on each step. "I fell overboard on a boat. The beaver knight who came here with me saved my life."

"Oh yes, Sir Brouglas," the seedling mused. "I heard about his exploits at Phranktonbourg. Powerful warrior."

"Um, I want him to be there when I take my oaths." They came to the top stair and Jab exhaled. "He taught me so much about Sprouterism. I don't think I would've been open to Ganan the Gardener, Blest be Him, without Sir Brouglas."

The seedling stepped in front of Jab. "You mean it? This is wonderful. I was looking for a reason to get him out."

"Get him out?" Jab asked.

The bent-whiskered mole rat nodded gravely. "He is to be executed. He insisted you and the other prisoners be set free. When we had the surprise arrival of Lady Marjitay and Sapling Galdwin, they told the baroness about how he'd betrayed the Frenglese nobility by putting in with Nasalid. They convinced her to execute him. But if you insist he must be the one to witness your oaths, I can delay his execution. It's a grave sin for them to refuse somebody from witnessing oaths."

The reality smacked Jab like a battering ram. Brouglas would get killed if he didn't do something right now.

32

SANU

Since you won't send enough funds to construct new battering rams, perhaps you'll allow me the use of your heads? I must warn you, the food at camp is horrible. The low quality has something to do with my stubborn princes and their lack of funds.

**- General Ironseed's third letter
to the Qawari princes**

Being involved with an army on the march was Sanu's dream when he was younger, yet now he was more concerned with how to *stop* this army.

Gizlee and Hunter described the injustices on Coppergrass, and the awful things that were said about Grovekeepers and Mulchers. Sanu's rage built. He didn't want this baroness to keep hurting the innocent rodents here. It didn't matter that they were on an island he'd only seen on maps. He remembered his burning desire to pick up a sword and defend the orphans in ZelZaytun when Nasalid besieged it, and now he was part of a besieging force.

After a few hours of traveling at an incline, the craggy hills flattened out, which Sanu realized was because they'd slowly climbed them. The castle came into view as they sloped off, and the speck in the distance caught a glint of the sun's glow, making him wonder how much of that stone fortress was laced with the island's copper. He wished Jab were somewhere far away from this cruel place, but upon spying the crenellations, Sanu understood deep within his bones that any captured person would be brought there.

Assuming they hadn't been killed immediately. The realization sank in his stomach and he sat uneasy on Korpin's horse. Even if he were still alive, if they destroyed this castle, Jab might get stuck inside.

Sanu checked over his shoulder and counted the carts of lumber which would be fashioned into siege weapons once they arrived. If there really was an army inside that castle, this battle would play out like a double siege game. He cast an eye at King Ridgerd. Sanu knew the hamster would go where the fighting was the toughest, pushing the battering ram into the gate and leading the charge inside. He wished Nett and Yagub were here instead of coaching the other seedlings in the back of the horde.

At Gizlee's suggestion, Ridgerd called for a halt. Sanu had to sit off to the side over the next hour as the preparations went underway.

Engineers and soldiers worked together, fashioning the lumber into a barricade, placing it over a carriage, affixing a chain, and readying the tree trunk that would make the actual ram piece.

Sanu needed to be inside that ram.

The barricade made a roof, sturdy enough to repel any arrows or stones from above. The roof was pointed, which meant he could hide inside its peak. The soldiers would be preoccupied with moving it forward and wouldn't notice him if he remained still. Then, once the gate was down, Sanu could sneak inside with the troops and search for his brother before Ridgerd ripped the castle apart. He owed it to his brother to at least try. For so much of his time on Coppergrass, he'd felt like he hadn't done enough to find Jab, and this might be his last opportunity. It was his only real lead so far, thanks to Gizlee.

Remembering her and Ridgerd speaking to each other on the march here gave Sanu an idea that might solve another problem.

He didn't know if they were interested in each other, but if they married, it would solve the issue of Ridgerd's bachelorhood. And in gratitude, they'd agree to call off the Qawar invasion. It was desperate, but nothing else had worked.

Something about playing matchmaker with two strangers didn't sit right, and if nothing else, the pair of them had other things to worry about.

Sanu found Hunter, who was staring at the castle in the distance. Amid the camp's noise, he could say anything and their conversation would be mostly private, even though rodents milled about.

"Hunter, can you tell me about my brother? How'd he seem?"

Hunter tore his gaze from the distant castle and sighed. "I thought he was older at first. Even now, I'm trying to remind myself that you and he are younger than me. He just seemed like he ... lived more, if that makes sense."

Sanu nodded slowly. Jab had lost his parents and spent months believing his twin was dead, all while preparing to attack the holiest place in the world and narrowly dodging death. If that counted as living, Jab was practically a senior citizen. Sanu wondered how old *he* seemed to everyone else.

But one thing still itched. "Did he seem ... happy?"

Hunter shrugged. "He had this look in his eye like he was searching for something. He wasn't miserable." After another sigh, Hunter added, "I was miserable enough for both of us. I'm sorry I ditched him."

Sanu faced the castle in the distance. "You were scared. And it sounds like a lot of unfair expectations were put on you." The truth was Sanu could scream at the spiny mouse, but he knew it wouldn't solve anything. It wouldn't bring Jab back. It wouldn't get anyone off this island, and it definitely wouldn't stop the invasion. He knew what he needed to do. "But you know what's better than an apology?"

"What?"

"Help me sneak inside the castle. If my brother is a prisoner, I need to get in before the fighting gets too intense and get him out of there. Your mom is the baroness, so how do I get in? I could sneak in with the battering ram, but there has to be an easier way, some secret passage."

Hunter found a new interest in his hind-paws. "I didn't grow up in that castle. Mom paid off the guards and they overthrew the old leader. I've only been in there a few times. I don't know where everything is or if there are secret passageways."

Sanu eyed the nearly-finished battering ram. "Make a distraction so I can sneak in there."

"In the ram? Are you crazy?" Hunter's outburst surprised Sanu. It was the most emotion he'd seen from him.

"No, I'm not crazy, I'm just out of time, ideas, and options. You *do* owe me for abandoning my brother. Unless you think you can get your mom to surrender."

The ram construction had finished, and the crew using it stepped inside, taking some practice swings. It wouldn't be long now. Sanu wondered if or how many backup rams the king would order, but if this survived the push to the gate, it might be able to knock it down.

"Now you really sound crazy." Hunter turned to face the army camp, where the soldiers who weren't working on the ram construction were busy drilling.

A stone's throw away, Ridgerd had gathered his top lieutenants, all of whom were older than him. Ridgerd gestured around the field, giving orders that Sanu couldn't hear over the noise of the camp.

"What are they saying?" Hunter asked.

Sanu knew. This was a game of double siege to him, but this time, the bait wouldn't be a general piece on the board, but a single rodent. The siege engines wouldn't come until the general and his vanguard had taken care of the main resistance. Taking down a single bandit was one matter, but the king was about to throw himself into the heat of battle against trained warriors.

And if Sanu perched inside the battering ram, he would see it all up close, and be in the most dangerous position.

As the hamster and his advisers continued their plans and more focus fell on them, Sanu tiptoed toward the battering ram.

33

JAB

Worried about Brouglas, Jab followed the seedling with a bent whisker through the castle to the inner courtyard, passing arches and tapestries. The courtyard had an interior garden, with stubby olive trees growing. Seeing the holy Gnaverwood in miniature felt comically wrong. A squadron of orange-black butterflies danced on the leaves. It would've looked serene and beautiful if not for the rodents gathered there.

In the center stood Baroness Bohbrat, flanked by the same guards who'd pushed Jab into prison. Beside her, Lady Marjitay and Sapling Galdwin looked smug. Between them, Brouglas the beaver knight, was stuck in stocks on wheels.

Jab's heart raced. The stocks held Brouglas in an arched kneeling position. If not torture, it looked humiliating.

The seedling pulled Jab forward. "Release that knight at once," bent whisker demanded.

Scowling, the Sapling approached. "You cannot speak that way to me. Your authority here is meaningless in my presence."

Lady Marjitay noticed Jab and grimaced. "He's a filthy spy from Qawar! One of Nasalid's rats."

Rat? Now that was just rude.

"I will take Sprouter vows," Jab said. "I want to be like you."

"You can't be serious," Marjitay said. "He's lying."

"I'm not," Jab lied. "Brouglas showed me that Ganan is good. Blest be Him."

The seedling placed a confident paw on Jab's shoulder. "We won't deny him the right to take the vows. He deserves to be at an Offering Meal with the one who showed him Ganan's light, Blest be Him."

Galdwin shook his head. "I do not authorize this."

The seedling tugged on his bent whisker. "You don't have to." Reaching into his tunic, he pulled out a gold-plated acorn hanging on a chain. An emerald sat in place of the stem. Jab had seen something similar in ZelZaytun; the girl Sanu liked, Cladh, had one. "You see," Bent Whisker continued, "our Sapling is visiting the Arborist in Gananshire, and I was entrusted to speak with her authority. Release the knight. He must attend the boy's initiation. You all have complained about the sins of King Ridgerd cursing Coppergrass. Refusal to allow the knight would tempt the All-Planter's wrath."

"Unacceptable," Lady Marjitay hissed.

From the stocks, Brouglas spoke in a strained voice. "Baroness, Lady Marjitay murdered Olihort's last Sapling. She's in league with Galdwin to undermine King Ridgerd. You cannot trust her."

Baroness Bohbrat massaged the sides of her head in tight circles. "We compromise. The beaver remains as he is and goes to this afternoon's Offering Meal to sit with the boy before he takes the vows. I'll station a guard behind them so they don't do anything untrustworthy."

Jab pushed forward so he could stand beside Brouglas. A guard threatened him with a devilbeak, but Jab didn't care. He glared at Lady Marjitay, then turned to the baroness. "I know why ZelZaytun fell. She made bad choices. I hated Sprouters because I thought they were like her. Brouglas showed me the truth."

"He lies!" Marjitay spat. "The beaver is a weakling and the squirrel is Qawar trash. I protected Olihort! Nasalid used Mulcher witchcraft and demons to steal the city from me."

The baroness called back her guard and examined Jab, then cast an eye at Marjitay.

Brouglas whispered in Qawari. "You mean it? You want to be a Sprouter?"

No. "Yes," Jab whispered back. He hated deceiving the good beaver, but he didn't have another option.

A guard mumbled something to Baroness Bohbrat, who then announced, "The boy is telling the truth. Move the knight to the Gananshed."

Jab's heart twisted. His lies might have saved one life. But he still needed to free his friend.

Traversing the castle's hallways a second time felt much different since the stocks had to be wheeled through. It reminded Jab of pulling Rijat's cart back home after he and Sanu buried their parents. The kindly gerbil had let them use his cart so they could carry the shovels and mourn their parents in private. If they hadn't died of the plague, more mourners would've come, and maybe Jab and Sanu wouldn't have had the fight which started them going off in separate directions all those months ago.

Brouglas lost his footing and Jab had to help him stand again. Guilt wiggled through Jab, realizing he'd thought so much of rodents dead and buried that he'd ignored the good beaver suffering beside him. All he'd accomplished was delaying Brouglas's death. Jab wouldn't stand for it. He'd find a way to save him, no matter what.

As the creaky wooden wheels squeaked through the castle, disgusted rodents averted their eyes from Brouglas and mischievous ones smiled at the seedling. Jab felt invisible, which he didn't mind.

The part of the castle leading from the courtyard and into the Gananshed felt much less like it was preparing for war and more as if it were meant to inspire religious awe. The hallway ended at a set of glass doors, colored like he'd seen in ZelZaytun, with a mosaic that would've been breathtaking in the sunshine.

The seedling opened the door and waved Jab and Brouglas inside.

"Is this your first Offering Meal?" the seedling asked.

Jab nodded. "I've been curious for a long time. My parents said awful things about Sprouters because you eat olives."

Brouglas breathed heavy in the stocks and fidgeted. "He's never had one before. Grovekeepers don't eat them."

"I know, sir knight," the seedling replied patiently.

Jab's mouth dried. Lying was one thing, but eating something his religion forbade felt even worse. His paws grew clammy with nervous sweat. He had to find some way not to take it if offered. "I-I'm not sure if I'm ready to eat one."

"Good." The seedling strode ahead toward a wooden pew, a partial bench with openings in the back that could accommodate any type of tail.

"Excuse me?" Jab jogged to catch up.

"You're just here to observe, my child—you know, I haven't gotten your name yet."

"Jab of Rattin."

Brouglas groaned behind them, and Jab doubled back to push him forward.

"I'm sorry I couldn't get you released." Bent whisker pointed to a spot near the wall where Jab could set Brouglas. An image in the wall's stone depicted scenes of what Jab assumed were images from Sprouter myths and hero stories. He wondered how many of these were representations of Mulcher stories that Grovekeepers believed in also. He would've liked to study each one and learn the history behind them, but knowing there were suffering prisoners below them, Jab had to focus. There had to be something in this prayer space that could help him get Brouglas released.

In the back, a table too tall for chairs sat upon a raised platform. Behind it sat a metal container, decorated in gold and copper, depicting Ganan's Rake and other symbols and Frenglese words Jab could only guess at. Knowing some phrases in Frenglese was not the same as spelling or reading them, especially considering the different alphabets. Beside the decorative container were candlesticks, shaped into rakes.

Jab pointed to the container. "What's in there?"

"Slices of olives from the sacred tree. Eating them is part of our prayer. The All-Planter commands it. By taking a bit of the sacred tree into ourselves, it reminds us to become better versions of ourselves. If a piece of the All-Planter is inside me, then I should act like it at all times." The seedling turned to Brouglas. "And I know Ganan, Blest be Him, would've done everything to get you out of that device."

The candlesticks looked sturdy enough that they might be able to break the stocks. He just needed to get the seedling out of here.

Behind them, the door burst open, and a troop of maids and cooks ran inside.

"What's going on?" the seedling asked, rising from the bench. "The Offering Meal isn't for another hour."

"We're sorry!" a maid called. "But the watchers spotted an army outside. They carry the banner of King Ridgerd!"

Jab's eyes widened. This was no time for a battle.

34

SANU

Dealing with you lot has made me regret my promotion. Twenty years ago, I would've swung a club and scimitar with the real heroes on the front, yet fate has reduced me to winning this war for you. In your last response, you said that I would win if it's the All-Planter's will. That may be true, but I will lose if you do not send more supplies.

*- General Ironseed's third
letter to the Five Princes*

This was the perfect time for a battle.

The troops marched forward at King Ridgerd's command. The hamster raised his sword aloft. "Do you want a speech?" he shouted, "Or do you want to defeat a tyrant and free our lost brothers?"

Shouts rose up and men banged on their shields and shook their spears and devilbeaks. Even the soldiers manning the battering ram paused to cheer, giving Sanu his one opportunity.

He darted inside, hopping onto the metal-capped tree trunk suspended by chains. Sanu scurried up a chain and latched onto the inner rafter of the high pointed ceiling. This contraption almost resembled a house with its pointed roof. But the metal plating would deflect any arrows or crossbow bolts and stay intact if any fire rained down.

He hoped.

The soldiers returned to the ram and pushed, safe from the battle that would commence outside thanks to its slanted roof. Ridgerd was running ahead with his elite troops, creating a diversion away from the ram. Enemy soldiers seeking glory would flock to the king, providing cover for the ram to get to the castle's gate.

Below Sanu, a row of devilbeaks hung on the inner wall, a last desperate defense for the ram if the soldiers needed to halt and clear out troops.

The engine moved forward, threatening Sanu's grip. The roof had enough of an opening for Sanu to observe the field before him. Ridgerd's troops weren't marching up an empty field leading to a castle, but approaching another army. Sanu squinted at the other side.

He recognized the banners they carried, showing the bighorn sheep with crossbow horns symbol. As they neared, it appeared as if the symbols were only recently stitched on, covering something else.

This must be all those town guards called out of Newhouse City and Rado Town and any other populated areas across the island. The baroness must have anticipated someone would rise up against her, but Sanu knew she couldn't have prepared for this. Nobody could prepare for King Ridgerd.

Sanu expected the approaching army to bank left and go for the king, but instead they came straight ahead for the battering ram. He wanted to shout at the soldiers steering and pulling to watch out and arm themselves, but he also couldn't afford to give away his position.

Ahead, King Ridgerd and his vanguard veered and met the defenders head-on.

Because of the ram's plodding pace, the king was a good deal in front. Warriors swarmed him, but the king batted them away with his sword, and nobody got close. For every soldier one of his troops engaged, Ridgerd had already knocked out two more fighters. His two-pawed sword sailed through the air, cutting and slashing and catching glints of sunlight. Even when enemies surrounded him, Ridgerd's size made him easy to notice.

But even that wasn't enough. More soldiers charged the ram, and the battle would be right in Sanu's face. The castle's walls loomed close enough to block out the clouds and cast the ram in shadow. The pushing team just needed a little more to get to the moat.

The soldier at the front called for a halt. "Grab yer devilbeaks, lads. It's time."

"No!" The shout came from King Ridgerd, who was running over, despite an attacker hanging from his back. The king shifted his sword grip to one paw and yanked the enemy off him, throwing the hapless fighter into a comrade. The hamster's facial fur was matted with blood and sweat. "Keep going, men!"

"Yes, my king!" the front soldier said below. The ram moved again, and the king engaged the attackers.

The ram plodded by Ridgerd, who was panting from the effort. Sanu dared to peek out again from his hiding spot, and a sick feeling rose inside him, realizing that his weight was adding to that of the ram and he was slowing them down. The ram might have gotten to the gates by this point, which would've meant fewer losses. All around, soldiers were falling. Ridgerd drew the attackers and defenders to himself like a whirlpool slurping in everything around it.

"Protect the ram!" the king bellowed, voice hoarse from battle. They were close enough now to the castle that arrows and crossbow bolts began to crash down, banging into metal armor and connecting with the ground and the creatures on it.

One arrow streaked toward Sanu's hiding spot, and he had to hug tight to the rafter. His fingers screamed at him to let go, but he needed to hold on a little longer.

Another volley of arrows descended, darkening the sky for a second. The two soldiers pushing the ram in front fell as wild arrows dug into their knees, then stumbled outside and crawled away from the fight.

They'd go even slower now.

"No!" Ridgerd bellowed again, and Sanu felt it in his bones. The king ran inside the ram and pushed, digging his hindpaws into the ground with each step, and it moved faster than when the other two soldiers were there. Whether that was from Ridgerd's added strength or from the inspiration in the other troops, Sanu couldn't know.

More arrows rained down, but they bounced off Ridgerd's higher-quality armor. A defender rushed the ram, but Ridgerd grabbed his sword with one paw and slashed him away.

Sanu maneuvered to the other side of the roof and got a better look at the defender. It was a porcupine. He hadn't seen a single one on Coppergrass Island, but there were plenty of them in Freng.

These weren't island natives.

These other soldiers were Frenglese, attacking Ridgerd who'd come to save them.

Sanu examined the battlefield behind them, noticing where the skirmishes had happened. The king wasn't killing them. He was fighting them until they gave up.

"Now, lads!" Ridgerd roared.

Sanu turned back around. Arrows *plinked* against the ram's metal roof, denting the inside but not penetrating.

They'd reached the gate. The soldiers inside dropped their handles and grabbed the pegs on the metal-capped trunk.

On the king's signal, they shoved it against the gate, and the reverberation shook Sanu more than he'd expected. With the second swing, Sanu fell.

35

JAB

Sprouters and Mulchers pray and fast too. How can they be far from the All-Planter's heart? Do not try to convert them by telling them they're wrong and will go to the Droughtlands when they die. Love them and treat them like the brothers that they are. Maybe they'll never change, but you still made a friend.

- Raticenna's collected sermons

The enemy threatened the gates.

Jab remembered the siege of ZelZaytun and watching the outer walls fall by the power of Nasalid's catapults. Rodents might have screamed inside the city that day, shouting the same thing about Jab and all the rodents with him.

Now Jab was the one on the inside of a besieged castle. He wouldn't die here. He refused. Brouglas wouldn't either. And bent whisker had risked Galdwin's wrath by believing Jab's lie. They all deserved better.

Jab tugged on the seedling's sleeve. "What is the bluntest and least holy thing in here?"

"Excuse me?" Bent whisker stepped back, mouth agape. The maids and cooks who had run inside flocked around the mole rat.

"Sir Brouglas is a fighter. I'm going to break him out of his stocks."

One of the cooks produced a kitchen knife from his belt. "I will cut the ropes around his hindpaws."

"The candlesticks aren't blessed," bent whisker said. "Bang those on the stockades. Enough good hits and the wood will break."

Two maids hustled over to the raised table and grabbed the candlesticks. The younger of the two smashed away at the corner of Brouglas's restraints and the older one handed the candlestick to a servant.

Jab wanted to do this himself, not involve everyone in his plan. He didn't know how much time they had, and he hated the idea of them risking their lives.

With pounds and grunts amid flying splinters, the broken stockades clattered to the floor and Brouglas stood.

"Thank you," the beaver said, stretching. "I will protect you. I will tell the attackers that you are just staff."

The chef turned his kitchen knife in his paw and gave it to the knight. "You'll need this more than me."

Brouglas faced the seedling. "I wish I could repay your kindness. But I must ask, do you have a blessed olive slice that I might have?" His voice lowered. "If I fail here, I wish for that to be my final taste."

"Of course," the seedling said. As he approached the metal container on the raised table, Brouglas spoke to Jab in Qawari.

"Your brother. He wanted to defend orphans when ZelZaytun was attacked by Nasalid. I want to be like him."

The seedling returned. After muttering something in a language Jab didn't understand, bent whisker displayed a shallow plate with a sliced olive on it and placed it gently in Brouglas's paw.

The beaver ate it, and a calm washed over his face. Such a tiny morsel couldn't possibly be satisfying, and yet the knight acted as if he'd just been given a glorious feast. "Jab, stay in here. I will give my all to defend you if the walls fail."

Jab turned to the chef. "Do you have another knife? I know how to fight. I'll help him."

Startled, the chef produced a smaller knife and passed it over, mumbling something that Jab thought meant, "He looks too young."

Knife in paw, Jab gave a thankful bow to the chef before turning to Brouglas. "They'll be safe with you. But there are other prisoners."

"What?" Brouglas asked.

Jab sprinted for the still-open doors. This knife would give him a chance to pick or break the locks holding the cells below. He'd paid close enough attention to the castle's twists and turns.

Some part of him wanted to bump into Lady Marjitay and Galdwin so he could tell any attackers where they were, but he pushed the thought from his mind. As he navigated the castle, soldiers ran through the halls in opposite directions, grabbing arrows and crossbow bolts and lining up by the arrow slits in the castle walls. They either didn't notice Jab or didn't care.

Upon arriving at the castle's main entrance, Jab found a troop of tense guards in attack formation, holding devilbeaks, surrounding the double doors in a semicircle. Anyone going through those doors would have a nasty surprise waiting for them. Jab ran by them and headed downstairs. Past winding corridors and spiraling stairs, Jab arrived at the cell blocks.

Huffing with effort, Jab heaved open the heavy oak door.

The old jerboa noticed him. "It's the young convert. We thought you'd abandoned us."

"Not on purpose," Jab replied. "Things got complicated upstairs."

"Lying does that to a soul," another inmate heckled. "Complications follow the liar like a stink on bad cheese."

Jab held up the knife. "I don't suppose any of you were ever thieves and know how to pick locks?"

"The liar wants a thief," the heckler said.

"Don't worry about that old fart." The jerboa pointed at the wall near the door where a key ring sat.

Jab grabbed the key ring and set about opening the old jerboa's cell.

"I'll get the others," the old timer said. "Thank you for freeing me. Now go, escape."

"Enemy soldiers are here," Jab said.

One of the other prisoners pressed his head against the bars. "Nasalid? The Liberator came for us?"

"No, it's the army of King Ridgerd," Jab said, "and he is close."

"Then you really need to escape," the jerboa whispered. "If it's not Nasalid, we are surely doomed."

36

SANU

*- General Ironseed's reprimand
to a failed sergeant*

S anu fell onto the battering ram trunk hard on his back, and he slid off into the arms of a confused soldier.

"A child?" the rattled beaver gasped.

Sanu scrambled out of the soldier's arms, trying to ignore the throb in his spine.

"Sanu?" Ridgerd bellowed. "What are you doing?"

Standing atop the metal cap, Sanu braced for a jump onto the gate. "I'm finding my brother."

"Get down!" the king barked.

"You're not my king," Sanu said as he took flight. He caught the iron gate's bars, and the hard metal made his fingers throb. He crawled into the opening, where he wriggled inside the gatehouse. Archers stood inside, raining arrows down below. If they spotted him, he'd be in big trouble.

But that would also mean they'd stop firing at the soldiers and focus on him.

The gatehouse shook, meaning the king continued his assault. Sanu wondered if this meant Ridgerd was trying to knock Sanu loose so he would fall to "safety" or because he wanted to press the attack. Either way, Sanu took it as his signal to get out.

The archers were still preoccupied, regaining their balance after the shock of the ram strike, and that's when Sanu spotted something precarious. A black cauldron full of bubbling hot liquid. If that poured down, all those soldiers could be melted alive. Nobody stood beside it, too focused on the arrow storm. They must be saving the cauldron for when the gate collapsed under the battering ram. Sanu wanted to push it to the opposite window and pour it over the side where nobody would get hurt. It was too big for him to move.

Although, it had wheels.

Sanu ducked behind it and set to work prying off one wooden wheel on his side. The gatehouse rocked below; another ram strike. The cauldron wobbled. That wasn't good.

Sanu pushed against the brim with his tail to keep it upright, and the blistering heat begged him to stop. But if he didn't do this, soldiers would boil in their armor. He couldn't let that happen. He could take a little heat. Sanu pried off the first wheel and placed it under the base to keep it from tipping onto him. As he worked on the second, another smack came against the gate.

The cauldron wobbled again, this time spilling some of its contents onto his tail and arm. He gritted his teeth and did his best not to yelp at the burn. He pried off the second wheel and plopped both into the cauldron. The bubbling golden oil crept over the wood, then hissed and smoked. Sanu's eyes widened. The soldiers stopped firing and turned around, staring straight at him and the fire.

"Pour it on them before it falls!" a soldier shouted.

The soldier had mistaken him for one of them, a page or squire or something. Sanu took the opportunity to run to the window sill looking out to the outer yard between the gate and the keep's main doors. Sanu braced himself to jump.

The gatehouse rocked again, and Sanu lost his balance. He tumbled toward the ground, painfully knocking against the stone wall. He thought walking with a bad ear had been difficult. He couldn't imagine walking around tomorrow after getting battered like this. As Sanu fell, he reached out with his paws and tail to grasp at anything. His tail caught a metal handle on the inside of the gate. Though he slipped and lost his grip, the handle had come down with his weight.

A *racka-click* came as a chain lifted. The lowered lever, along with the ram smacking the gate, had loosened something in the mechanism.

As the metal warped, the gate flew open.

Sanu rolled out of the way, and the gate he'd just climbed lay beside him on the ground.

"Sanu!" Ridgerd bellowed. "Get back inside where it's safe."

Sanu scrambled to his hindpaws and sprinted forward. He was getting inside that castle before the king if it was the last thing he ever did. He pushed himself, and arrows rained down from the keep, aimed at the ram. They weren't shooting at him. Maybe the soldiers inside the castle had mistaken Sanu for one of theirs as well. He reached the double doors and they opened a crack.

A soldier in Frenglese armor poked his head out. "Come in!" he hissed.

Sanu's eyes widened. This had to be a trap, but he didn't know another way inside.

"We saw you flee the gatehouse. We didn't know Sir Brouglas was stationed up there." He ushered Sanu inside, where a troop of guards with devilbeaks stood at the ready. The soldier who let him in closed the door behind Sanu and another pulled a locking bar down. "We saw you come into the keep with him earlier, but nobody has seen him."

Sanu's heart raced. Sir Brouglas was in this castle somewhere, and so was Jab.

While he was relieved at the soldiers' mistake, the thought struck him. His brother may have decided that Ridgerd was an enemy worth fighting. Maybe Jab was the reason these soldiers were taking up arms against their king.

He needed to act fast. "Is the baroness here?" Sanu hoped he sounded like Jab. "I have a message for her."

"Wait," one of the guards said. "Didn't this kid get tossed in the cells? I thought they said Brouglas's kid was a Grovekeeper."

The other soldiers lowered their weapons and glared at Sanu.

Maybe resembling his twin wasn't so lucky after all.

37

JAB

- Divine Poetics

While the old jerboa freed the other inmates, Jab sprinted up the stairs. He wasn't sure what he'd expected, but he wondered why he hadn't felt the castle falling apart. Catapults hurling rocks at the walls would've shaken the basement, right? Maybe the servants were wrong and the castle wasn't under attack, but that wouldn't explain the soldiers at the door. He did not want to tangle with them.

He reached the top of the stairs, arriving on the main floor. Defenders manning the arrow slits in the walls fired their volleys, and he realized his only escape through the castle would be to distract the guards or find some way to escape the roof. Too bad he couldn't fly.

The thought of a flying squirrel made him chuckle, but he shook his head. No time for silliness.

He rounded the corner and climbed the steps, but the main entrance opening caught his attention.

Jab stopped in his tracks like he'd hit an invisible wall and his heart fell to his stomach.

Sanu was here.

And whatever journey he was on had not been kind. He was missing a chunk of his ear and he looked ragged.

Sanu said something to the guards, who went back and forth for a moment, but then they aimed their weapons at him.

Jab wasn't about to let his brother go down. For Sanu to arrive here meant he must've crossed the whole island searching for him. Jab needed to do something.

He knew what would catch their attention.

"Large life, King Ridgerd!" Jab shouted in Frenglese, hoping he said it right.

The guards' attention snapped to Jab, and one of them pointed up at him. "That's the real one!" a guard shouted.

Jab was quite pleased with himself for the split second before guards started chasing him, and he bolted up the stairs.

Two guards restrained Sanu.

That wasn't good. All of them were supposed to give chase, but Sanu remaining tied up wouldn't do Jab any favors. He needed to rescue his brother.

Reaching the top of the steps to the second floor, Jab spied the banner from before, the long flowing one that held the baroness's symbol.

After his treatment in her care, he didn't mind defacing it. Jab leapt off the banister and sank his claws into the fabric, slicing a path down for him to safely get back to the floor.

The flowing banner came with him, and Jab jumped through it, bounding toward the door where his brother was. Fighting two guards wasn't within Jab's ability, but he didn't have to. There must be a real army outside, otherwise the archers wouldn't be firing through slits. They might not be using catapults, but they were close enough.

Jab neared the door, and one of the soldiers restraining Sanu released him and chased Jab.

The other guards who'd run up the stairs were descending. They'd all be on him in seconds. Jab hopped onto the bar blocking the entrance, then he had nowhere to go. The nearest soldier lunged for him with his bare paws. He'd dropped his weapon.

Skipping out of the way, Jab called out to his brother. "Get that devilbeak!"

Sanu writhed against the soldier's grip, and used his tail as a lever to push himself away while Jab jumped on the edge of the locking mechanism, letting it come up. The blocking bar slid up from Jab's weight on its end, and he ran down the last few inches so it would stand up completely.

Shoulder first, Sanu rammed into the left door, letting it swing open, revealing a battering ram plodding toward the entrance.

"That's where we need to go," Sanu said.

Jab wished the first words they'd shared could've been more friendly and meaningful, but he was glad to hear his brother's voice again.

"Brouglas is inside the castle!" Jab hissed as he dodged one of the guards' attempts to grab him.

"He'll be fine," Sanu replied, running out the door.

Jab watched his brother as he dodged more strikes from the guards. The other soldiers were back down the stairs and running after them.

Outside, the ram had slowed, because one of the rodents inside had left it.

It was King Ridgerd, blocking arrows with a kite shield in one arm, while carrying a sword any other rodent would've needed two paws for.

The hamster was leading a charge against this castle, and the other soldiers were trying to keep up.

"Sanu!" Ridgerd shouted. "Get behind me!"

Sanu ran toward the colossal hamster, and Jab followed.

Arrows flew from all directions, and one grazed Jab's tail. It hurt, but the bleeding wouldn't be as bad as the beaver knight's was.

Once he was close enough to hear Ridgerd's breathing, Jab called to him, "Brouglas is inside. Please keep him safe."

Without breaking stride or making eye contact, King Ridgerd uttered, "I swear it."

The battering ram had slowed again, but this time it was because other soldiers were running through in pairs, each one holding a shield up to block arrows. They couldn't outrun the king.

Jab hugged the side of the passage wall, watching for arrow fire and letting the soldiers pass him.

These men seemed identical to the ones who'd crash landed here. All it took was believing gossip for people to take different sides.

But there was one truth he'd seen that nobody could contradict. King Ridgerd was a force of nature. Anyone who fought him would have better luck fighting the weather. New dread bubbled in Jab's gut, remembering that Qawar was next on Ridgerd's list.

Jab and Sanu locked eyes as pairs of knights ran between them.

They'd reunited, but for better or worse, this castle was about to get annihilated, and Coppergrass would never be the same. Any victory here would eventually spell doom for Qawar.

38

SANU

Breathing heavy and wincing from a fresh reminder of his damaged ear, Sanu locked eyes with Jab. He'd come so far to find him, and yet he felt like he didn't recognize his brother; Sanu had the physical scar, but Jab seemed to carry something on the inside. Soldiers rushed past them. They couldn't go inside and risk getting hit, and if they stayed put they were just as likely to get trampled.

"We have to find Nett," Sanu called. "She and the seedlings can stop this."

Another arrow flew in front of Jab. "There are archers in the windows all over that castle. We'll get—" Jab backed away as a soldier charged past. "We'll get an arrow through the skull if we are too noticeable."

"Then try not to get trampled," Sanu replied. "Finding the seedlings is all that matters."

On opposite sides of the walkway, the brothers raced toward the ravaged gatehouse. Sanu wondered how many soldiers had given their lives in this attack already and hated himself for wishing any calamity on Ridgerd's army. Maybe they could dethrone that awful baroness and call Ridgerd's sacred debt paid.

Past the gatehouse, the field lay littered with groaning soldiers, writhing in the grass.

Gizlee knelt over one, applying salve to a cut.

"Gizlee!" Jab shouted.

The hamster turned toward him and her eyes widened. "There's our hero. We were worried you'd been taken here."

"Who's 'we'?" Jab asked.

Sanu's heart sank remembering that Hunter had apparently betrayed Jab and Brouglas, even though he'd later had a change of heart. Jab wouldn't know that.

"The good rodents of Rado Town," she replied. Standing, she gestured to other rodents who were tending the injured. "We aren't fighters, but we do know how to help."

Sanu appraised Gizlee. She would definitely want to stay on Coppergrass if Ridgerd was successful today. She would want to be with the locals and help them recover. "What do you think of King Ridgerd?" Sanu asked.

Jab arched an eyebrow, giving him a confused look.

"I met him only recently. I don't understand why you'd ask with a battle raging." She blinked a few times, then turned her attention back on Jab. "Hunter is very sorry for what he did. If he hadn't come back and confessed to us though, we never would've found you."

Jab stared at his hindpaws, and Sanu placed a paw on his shoulder.

But Sanu needed to know. "What would you think about marrying the king?"

"It never occurred to me. I also *only met him very recently.*" Gizlee pointed to the writhing soldier on the ground and applied more salve. "Boys, I'm happy to see you both, but I must tend the wounded."

Sanu winced. "Sorry. Do you know where the seedlings are?"

Gizlee pointed over her shoulder with her thumb, indicating a tent. "They set up there to pray over the wounded and give final blessings to the fallen."

"Thank you." Sanu grabbed Jab's wrist and ran toward the tent.

"Why do you need the seedlings?" Jab asked.

"A bunch of bad seedlings convinced Ridgerd he's going to the Droughtlands unless he takes ZelZaytun from Nasalid. If the good ones here all bless Ridgerd's victory, then he might lose some pressure to fight in Qawar. And they can broker a peace, I hope."

"There's a good seedling in the castle," Jab said. "But there's one more problem."

They stopped in front of the tent and caught their breath. Sanu's ear burned. "What do you mean?"

"Lady Marjitay and Sapling Galdwin. They're in the castle."

The twins locked eyes, and Sanu knew Jab was remembering being witness to Lady Marjitay murdering the good Sapling of ZelZaytun when she refused to surrender.

"What are you doing?" a feminine voice cut through their pondering. It was Nett. She gasped. "You found your brother!"

Sanu nodded. "This is Jab, and he has information that needs to get to King Ridgerd."

"Hello, Jab." Nett wiped her paws on her apron. "This is the problem with the king's fighting style. We can't bring him news when he's in the front. What does he need to know?"

Jab took a deep breath and glanced at Sanu. Sanu motioned for Jab to start talking.

"The Sapling Galdwin and Lady Marjitay are inside the castle. They will kill everyone who stands against them, and they are good at persuading the baroness. The baroness has also done awful things to the rodents of Coppergrass, most especially the Mulchers and Grovekeepers."

Sanu was impressed by his brother's ability to speak in Frenglese. Brouglas must have taught him. Stepping up beside Jab, Sanu added, "We need you to get the seedlings to the castle and call for a truce. The soldiers might not all listen to Ridgerd, but they would accept a seedling's orders, especially a group of them all saying the same thing."

"And their Sapling is away," Jab said.

The last of the soldiers had charged inside the castle. Sanu hoped if Brouglas was still in there, he could protect himself.

Light footsteps came from behind. "We'll go inside," a new voice said. "Together, protecting the seedlings."

Sanu spun around, and saw Yagub smiling back at him.

"It's good to see you, Jab," Yagub said. "I heard Sir Brouglas is in the castle. Where's Jandi?"

Jab shrugged. "He sank under all his armor, I think. Brouglas and I washed ashore together."

Yagub clenched his fists as the information sank in. "It's my sworn duty to protect him. I need to go."

Nett pushed her wrists against her hips. "We can't just up and leave. We have wounded and dying rodents in front of us who need care."

"What if you came by yourself?" Sanu asked. It wouldn't be the group of seedlings he'd wanted, but it would be better than nothing.

From inside the tent, two younger seedlings emerged. "Take our signs of oath," one said, reaching into his tunic. He pulled out a gold-plated acorn.

"Speak with our authority," the second said, giving her his own acorn.

"Come on," the first one said, turning back to the tent. "Our sister needs us, and we have to fulfill our duty to the sick."

Five more seedlings of various species and sizes exited, all clutching gold acorns.

Nett accepted them all with a bow and affixed them to her own chain. With a smile, she turned to the boys. "I suppose we should be off then?"

39

JAB

- Raticenna's commentaries on the Divine Poetics

Jab ran beside his brother, wondering what kind of tale was behind his damaged ear, and made an unofficial prayer of gratitude for his apparent recovery. Still, it must have hurt to lose a chunk of ear like that. And yet it did give him that toughened warrior look Sanu had wanted since he was a baby.

They neared Gizlee, who tended another wounded soldier, helping him to stand.

"Why did you ask her about King Ridgerd?" Jab asked.

Sanu looked at him before returning his focus forward. "The king is pressured to go to war. The Sapling is saying he'll be sent to the Droughtlands when he dies because of something he's done, and the only way the Sapling will ask the All-Planter to keep Ridgerd's soul out of the eternal punishment is to win back ZelZaytun."

Yagub and Nett glanced over their shoulders at them, but kept quiet.

"Nobody will tell me what Ridgerd did," Sanu continued, "but I think it's because he doesn't want to get married, which is bad for a king. But if he marries Gizlee and she stays on Coppergrass, I thought that would get everyone off Ridgerd's tail. He wouldn't be worried about the Droughtlands and he wouldn't have to continue the invasion."

Yagub slowed to a halt. "Nett? What do you think?"

Nett sighed and stopped along with Jab and Sanu. "I don't think King Ridgerd will be sent to the Droughtlands, but he's been convinced by judgmental saplings and seedlings that he will be unless he does what they want. I think it's awful."

"But what about my plan?" Sanu asked.

Nett looked over at Gizlee, who had gotten the soldier back on his hindpaws, and they started limping their way. "Madam Gizlee isn't a piece of property to be traded." She cast an eye at Yagub, and then the twins. "I don't know if the king would agree to it. And I don't know if anyone would believe it."

"Believe it?" Jab asked. What was to doubt? Public weddings of royals weren't exactly things people could just fake.

Nett sighed. "Let's ask."

Jab remembered that conversation between Gizlee and Brouglas a few days ago. "Madam Gizlee never wanted a husband. I overheard her explain it to Brouglas. Maybe she's never met the right man?"

"What's all this about me?"

Everyone's eyes snapped to the lady hamster who had a soldier's arm draped around her neck. "Do you mind giving me space?" Gizlee asked. "I need to get him to the seedlings."

Jab gazed at the soldier. He looked like he'd taken an arrow to the knee. He remembered Brouglas's injury.

Jab shook his head. "We'll ask later—"

"Please marry King Ridgerd!" Sanu blurted.

Jab covered his face with his paws. He'd forgotten his brother's gift of subtlety. "We haven't asked the king about it yet," he muttered.

"This is no time for marriage talk," Gizlee said, brushing past them.

As she walked away, Jab knew he should let her go. "I heard what you said to Sir Brouglas. Marrying King Ridgerd would silence everyone, and he'd never be here. It would be like you were still unmarried."

Gizlee huffed and flicked her nub of a tail in a way he didn't quite understand, but he did get the idea that it was not a happy movement.

"There. You tried," Nett said, "Now let's get into the castle. There will be time after the battle for the pair of them to discuss your plan."

Jab wondered what sins the king could've done to be hated or feared by so many, but then Jab remembered his own dishonest streak. Maybe all rodents carried a secret shame inside them.

They reached the gatehouse, which was a few stones thinner since the last time Jab had passed through it. The guards had gone, and it looked like they never had a chance to dump their burning oil, which sent a scorched odor through the air that reminded Jab of bad cooking.

Heading down the walkway, they passed more soldiers who had taken arrow fire and now had Rado Town villagers tending to them. As close as Jab and Sanu had come to losing their heads on this walkway, he found a deeper respect for these camp followers who were risking their own lives to tend to the wounded. A sudden fear gripped Jab that any archers in the windows would have a clean shot at them, but a glance to the castle revealed that no arrows flew. Whoever had been firing must have abandoned their post to fight the onrush of Ridgerd's soldiers.

The castle would stink of violence. A bad memory surfaced of Jab being forced to watch one of the battles leading up to the siege of ZelZaytun.

The crunch of bones. The desperate final shouts. The thud of clubs against metal armor. It had been a while since those memories had attacked his sleep, but now they weren't even bothering to wait for him to close his eyes. Jab breathed as slowly as he could for someone running, trying to calm himself.

Whatever waited for him inside, at least he had his brother by his side, which was more than he could say for his whole time on Coppergrass.

He needed Brouglas to be safe though. After losing his parents and Kash back on Qawar, he couldn't stand to lose another mentor here.

40

SANU

The twins passed through the double doors into the castle's main entrance, and the sight didn't match what Sanu saw only an hour ago. The soldiers who had stood guard were gone, and blood stained the carpet. The grand tapestry lay torn and tattered from Jab's earlier heroics.

Sanu turned to his brother. "Where's Sir Brouglas? Should we get him first?"

"Yes," Yagub said. "We have to make sure he's safe."

"That's not a priority," Nett grumbled. "We have to find the king before he does something rash."

Sir Brouglas had risked everything for Jab on Coppergrass and Sanu back in Qawar. While he wished to see the beaver right away, he hung his head. "Jab, you know where Brouglas is. You and Yagub can get him. Let's split up." The words hurt to say, since Sanu wasn't in a hurry to be away from his brother again, but both teens were right.

Jab nodded, and where Sanu had expected hurt, he found resolve in his brother's eyes. "The throne room is up those stairs. That's my best guess where the nobles are. If this battle is over or ending, that will be the final stand."

And where the fighting would be the toughest, Sanu knew. It was exactly where the king would go.

"Meet us there after you get Brouglas?" Sanu asked.

"Of course," Jab replied.

Sanu extended his arms, and Jab rushed into them. They hugged tight. "See you soon."

"Not if I see you first." Jab broke away and led Yagub down a hall.

"Come on," Nett said. "Let's head upstairs. We don't know what's happened yet."

Metal clangs echoed in the halls around them, along with different shouts in Frenglese. That didn't sound like the fight had ended at all.

Sanu and Nett hurried up the steps, and Sanu had to grip the banister tightly to keep his balance. His ear throbbed, and it was affecting his legs and coordination. He wasn't keen on falling down the cold stone steps either.

"I know you were at the siege of the Holy City," Nett said. "I don't know what you saw there, but this might be gruesome."

Sanu wasn't sure how to tell her that he'd seen death before. Sometimes when he closed his eyes, he still heard the screams. He'd tried not to think about it since coming to Coppergrass, but sleeping on the ship coming over here had been a nightly ordeal with nightmares. "We'll deal with it. Let's go."

They reached the steps' midpoint, and his paw slid over a crack in the banister. This was where a soldier had struck at Jab, missing him by inches with his devilbeak. His brother almost died here. But Jab had risked himself for Sanu. He was a good brother.

At the top of the steps, the clanging metal and shouts had dissipated, reduced to echoes. A set of double doors matching the ones at the entrance lay before them, hanging open. Inside, a host of rodents stood with swords and crossbows at the ready.

On one side stood King Ridgerd, breathing hard, with a pawful of soldiers around him. On the other side were a troop of heavily armored guards, all wielding devilbeaks or crossbows. Behind them, Sanu spied Lady Marjitay, Galdwin the Sapling, and a third rodent, a spiny mouse, dressed like a noble. That must be the baroness.

King Ridgerd stepped forward, shield at the ready. "Lay down your weapons. My troops are storming the castle. You stole this throne from my cousin and the long paw of justice has arrived."

From behind the troops, Lady Marjitay snarled back at him. "And you're a traitor. Attacking a friendly nation like Coppergrass."

"End this farce, Ridgerd, and attack Qawar," Sapling Galdwin said. "Your cousin was weak filth and let Mulchers and Grovekeepers poison this island. You're dooming yourself and our chances. What have you done to these innocent pilgrims of the All-Planter?"

King Ridgerd looked at the baroness. "Lady Marjitay murdered a Sapling and Galdwin abused his authority to cover it up." The hamster pointed his sword at her guards. "Is this what you wanted, lads? Do you think I'm some kind of devil? I came here to rescue you all. Have you heard what's happening on this island?"

"Kill him!" the baroness shouted.

Sanu saw which crossbowman had taken point. "On your left!"

The king ducked his shoulder down and a crossbow bolt sailed over his head. The king ran into the middle of the guards with devilbeaks, and Sanu bolted forward.

"Wait!" Nett begged.

Sanu knew firstpaw what a crossbow bolt could do, and he wasn't about to let the king get killed. Ridgerd's other soldiers charged after their king, and a melee started.

Those crossbows would be the deciding factor.

Sanu found his opening. This room also had a floor-to-ceiling tapestry bearing the baroness's coat of arms. With enough speed, Sanu might be able to climb up it. He had no other choice.

As he approached, the crossbowmen backed away, and Ridgerd went blow-for-blow with the guards.

Lady Marjitay turned in Sanu's direction. "Get the brat!"

The same crossbow holder who'd fired on King Ridgerd turned on Sanu and cranked his crossbow.

Racka-click

Sanu's balance was still off, and he couldn't run in a straight line, which was probably for the best as the crossbowman adjusted his aim.

"Sanu!" Ridgerd cried.

"Stop this, all of you!" Nett shouted, but nobody listened.

The soldier's aim steadied, and he fired.

Sanu dove to the floor, and the bolt took off a chunk of his tail fur.

"He's a boy!" Ridgerd roared. "You fired on a child! To the Droughtlands with you!"

Sanu glanced up. The guards Ridgerd had engaged lay sprawled on the floor, groaning. The king tackled the crossbowman, and the crunch of metal on bone echoed through the room as a stray crossbow bolt collided with the ceiling.

"Now," Ridgerd said, getting up. "We'll negotiate peace terms." The king kicked the soldier's dropped crossbow.

Nett had caught up, and she lifted her collection of acorns aloft. "I come here under the authority of ten seedlings. I'll mediate."

Sanu breathed hard, and the pain in his tail burned, but he collected himself and rose to his hindpaws.

The king had won.

41

JAB

- Divine Poetics

Yagub's presence didn't ease Jab's sense of dread. Running through the twisting halls toward the Gananshed, he hoped none of Ridgerd's soldiers would attack a holy place. He remembered Nasalid giving strict orders in the ZelZaytun siege: every building which wasn't specifically a military building must be left alone, but Jab wasn't sure if the hamster gave similar warnings. Memories of his mentor, Kash, with a devilbeak in his skull resurfaced, making Jab worry something similar had happened to Brouglas.

When Jab and Yagub reached the courtyard, they found signs of battle—broken arrows and torn-up grass. Fearing the worst, Jab turned toward the castle's Gananshed. Standing outside the double doors were Brouglas and bent whisker—the kind seedling Jab had lied to.

"Sir Brouglas!" Jab and Yagub cried at the same time.

The beaver laughed and flexed. "A few raiders came by, but instead of fighting them, I showed them what was inside and who. They checked and checked, but thankfully, we had nothing to hide."

Yagub dove in for a hug. "The battle is won. King Ridgerd's here."

"The good king," Brouglas intoned. "I missed you, Yagub."

Jab wanted to join them, but he needed to return to Sanu. "We have to get to the throne room. They're going to decide what'll happen to Coppergrass." Jab fixated on the seedling's symbol of authority, the gold-plated acorn he'd seen in ZelZaytun. "You both need to come."

"If the battle is truly over," the seedling mused, "then I suppose we should. I've heard stories of Prince Ridgerd. I'd love to see him as a king."

Bent whisker peeped inside the Gananshed and told the workers it was safe to leave, and then he proceeded to lead them to the throne room, taking a more direct route.

Climbing a set of stairs, Brouglas elbowed Jab. "I have something for you, boy." He pulled a thick book from his tunic. "It's our holy book. I'm... I'm really happy you decided to take the oaths."

Jab's mouth dried. "I..."

The seedling opened a door, and they came to a side entrance of the throne room, and Jab wondered how he hadn't noticed this door when he was in here earlier.

Brouglas tucked the book back into his tunic. "I'll give it to you later."

Jab gasped at the scene before them. Soldiers writhed on the floor; King Ridgerd pointed a sword at the baroness, the lady, and the Sapling; Sanu was nursing a bleeding tail.

"What is happening?" the seedling demanded.

Nett came forward. "We are negotiating a peace."

Lady Marjitay guffawed. "You can't touch us. The so-called 'murder' you want to blame on me did not have enough evidence. My word and the kind Sapling's are legal enough."

Brouglas clenched his fist, and Jab got an idea.

"Wait, King Ridgerd! What if you made Sir Brouglas a noble?" Jab couldn't believe the words coming out of his mouth. This wasn't the place for someone like him to talk, but it seemed like they were in a deadlock.

Brouglas's tail stiffened. "My liege, then my testimony would be more valid." He glared at the baroness. "I watched her murder the Sapling of Olihort."

Nett stepped forward, shaking her collection of acorn symbols. "I have enough authority with these to verify Sir Brouglas becoming a noble."

Bent whisker came between king and baroness. "And I carry my Sapling's authority with me. I can cancel out Galdwin's testimony."

King Ridgerd sheathed his sword and helped Sanu stand. "I will give Brouglas the land I will conquer. He'll be protector of Olihort."

"That's my title!" Lady Marjitay shrieked.

Jab grinned. Not anymore.

Galdwin seethed. "This doesn't change the matter of your eternal soul, Ridgerd. You'll be sent to the Droughtlands for your evil."

"And conquering Olihort is all I can do to appease the All-Planter," Ridgerd said.

A rock formed in Jab's stomach. This wasn't how it was supposed to go.

"Galdwin," Ridgerd said, closing the distance between them. "You will be sent to the Arborist in Gananshire with a full report of what you've allowed to happen. In that report, I'll explain how one of the conditions of my invasion is your removal from office." He glanced at Nett. "I have a fine idea of who to recommend the Arborist replace you with."

"You wouldn't dare," Galdwin hissed. "We'll tell everyone what you've done."

Ridgerd examined the room and sighed. "Go ahead. We believe the All-Planter will forgive. So I ask that everyone pray for me as I try to become more pure."

"We have a wife for you!" Sanu exclaimed.

Jab moved over to his brother. "We think you and Lady Gizlee would make a fine match."

"I'd like to know *her* stance on the matter first. We'll discuss that another time," Ridgerd said, looking a bit shocked. "And for you, *Baroness*, for your crimes against the good rodents of Coppergrass, you'll be replaced with Lady Gizlee.

Since she knew my dear cousin the best, she'll be able to rule in her memory. I'll take you all to the dungeons until we can arrange for proper transportation. Your children..." Ridgerd let the word hang in the air.

"What?" the baroness shouted. "You'll kill them, right? All I ever did was be a good mother."

"Your children will be pardoned," the king said. "I won't judge a teenager like an adult. They're young enough to deserve another chance."

42

SANU

I hope you enjoyed bickering instead of sending supplies and reinforcements. I regret surrendering, but the idea of your misguided rule coming to an end is a consolation. History will blame me, I'm sure you'll see to that, but the All-Planter knows the truth.

- General Ironseed's final
letter to the Five Princes

That night, Sanu and Jab were invited to the almost-clean throne room, where King Ridgerd stood by the throne. Gizlee occupied the opposite side, and they were flanked by Nett and the seedling Jab found—Sanu really wished Jab had told him that guy's name. Among the crowd inside the cavernous room were the now-unarmed soldiers who had defended the castle.

King Ridgerd shot them stern looks, and they responded by staring at their hindpaws or grimacing back at their king.

The king inhaled and waved toward Gizlee. "This fine woman shall lead Coppergrass in recovering from the baroness's desolation. I am not taking this throne for myself but restoring it to the Coppergrass rodents."

Relief pumped through Sanu, but a bigger part of him wished the king would stay and cancel the invasion.

"I extend you all pardon," Ridgerd continued, "and allow you to complete your pilgrimage to the holy island. Your criticisms of me were guided by a deceitful man. I wish to put all rumors to rest now."

Gizlee and Ridgerd exchanged a look of resignation. A knot formed in Sanu's gut. He didn't think these two could possibly have a happy marriage, based on that shared look, but neither one had seemed like the kind of rodent who wanted to marry anyway. He hoped his idea hadn't ruined their lives.

Ridgerd motioned toward Nett and the other seedling. "To put any rumors to rest, I'll show you all how earnestly I desire a queen." His voice was monotone, almost sad. "In all of Freng, I never found a woman who could steal my heart. Perhaps it was because the All-Planter wished for me to come here and meet you, Gizlee."

"Thank you, my king." Gizlee's monotone matched the king's.

Sanu remembered his parents expressing love for each other and describing the day they'd met. It sounded nothing like this.

The royal hamster nodded, and Nett and the seedling came to the center. "Lady Gizlee and I will marry here and now. Because I have the war to fight, and she has Coppergrass to restore, we will have to bid adieu for now." This time, when fiancée and fiancé exchanged a glance, it was from the side of their eyes and came with a tiny smirk. Sanu wouldn't have noticed if he hadn't been so close.

Nett opened a prayer book and recited. "As we all yearn to grow and garden like our dear Ganan,"

"Blest be Him," came the chorus from the crowd.

"—so we celebrate the sprouting of a new family. One which may be blessed with happiness." Nett hesitated for a half-second. "—and children."

Ridgerd's whiskers stiffened. "We pray for both."

Gizlee nodded. "We pray for both."

"Do you both understand the demands of marriage? Do you both know the sacrifices you will need to make for the other?"

"We do," they said in unison.

Each second they didn't smile brought a new stab of guilt into Sanu. This wasn't the joyous ritual he'd expected, and the king would continue his war anyway. Sanu wanted to scream for it to stop, but he glanced over his shoulder at the soldiers behind him.

They were smiling.

They weren't close enough to see the tiny facial expressions or they hadn't spent enough time with their king to know his quirks. At least they wouldn't betray him again.

"Then, by the All-Planter's grace and Lord Ganan's guidance,"

"Blest be Him."

"I pronounce you king and queen. Enjoy your first kiss."

King Ridgerd hugged Gizlee tight. He was so much taller than her that it was comical and awkward to see them kiss.

Jab nudged Sanu. "Hey," he whispered in Qawari, "they just kissed on the cheek."

Sanu arched an eyebrow. "Aren't they supposed to kiss on the lips?"

"Maybe it's different from Grovekeeper weddings," Jab mused. "Maybe that's why they don't sound happy either."

Sanu whispered, "maybe," but his single word was overwhelmed by the chorus of cheers from the gathered soldiers. Whatever they had once believed about their king had been put to rest.

The king pulled away and plastered a smile on his face. "Now I hope you are all satisfied. Because we have brothers to mourn and a castle to repair, we'll spare the expenses of a formal celebration tonight. Your king commands you all to get a good night's rest."

The next day, Sanu and Jab finished their afternoon prayer together, and sat beside each other in the shipyards near the castle. The transport ship that had blown off-course was getting its repairs, and another vessel was being loaded up—one with the former Sapling Galdwin, the former Lady Marjitay, and the former Baroness Bohbrat.

Sanu didn't know what fate awaited them, but any prison sentence felt too generous. While it was a relief to know these foul rodents wouldn't plague Sanu's life anymore and they wouldn't ruin any more islands, the hard truth surfaced.

Jab sighed. "I hope our trip to Qawar is long and detoured again. I can't wrap my head around the fact that we failed."

"I don't know if it's a total failure," Sanu replied. "The Mulchers and Grovekeepers of Coppergrass got their rights back."

Jab pointed to the former nobles boarding the ship bound for Gananshire. "And those three won't be able to hurt anyone anymore."

Sanu turned to Jab. "But you know what this means, right?"

"That we're done with the Honking Goose?" Jab smiled.

"No," Sanu replied, voice darkening, "We still have one enemy left."

"Who?"

Who else? A tear rose to the surface and spiders tickled Sanu's insides. "King Ridgerd."

His hero. The king who had saved this island now set his sights on their home.

And he'd shatter it.

King Ridgerd is on the warpath and Nasalid will defend Qawar to the last. With ties to both sides, how will Sanu and Jab bring about peace? See who emerges the victor in the final installment of the trilogy, coming soon! Or if you need more rodent madness in another part of the Great Sea, check out the *Ghosts and Iron* series!

BOOK CLUB QUESTIONS

1. How did Brouglas and Ridgerd change Sanu and Jab's perspectives?

2. In the last book, Nasalid struggled with his troops not wanting to follow him, and Ridgerd had a similar problem here. What do you think makes for a good leader?

3. Did your opinion of either brother change from the first book? Why?

4. Sanu and Jab are terrified of their home being destroyed when Ridgerd invades Qawar. What were the other "shattered homes" they saw on this adventure and how did that affect them?

5. Do you think Jab went too far in telling lies or was he doing the right thing? Explain.

6. Sanu and Jab met some helpful friends and dangerous foes in their journeys. Which side character was your favorite and why?

7. Why do you think it was important to see religious leaders who were kind and cruel to Ridgerd?

8. Was Sanu right to follow and stick up for Ridgerd even though Ridgerd wants to invade Sanu's home? Explain.

9. What was your favorite part of the book?

10. What are your predictions for when Sanu and Jab sail home?

AUTHOR BIO

PC is a fantasy and science fiction author from the Great Lakes region of the USA. Fantasy has been a deep love for PC, growing up on Star Wars movies and reading the Redwall series. The Star Wars novels along with fantasy greats like Brandon Sanderson, C.S. Lewis, and Tolkien are constant sources of inspiration and wonder. PC loves taking his daughters to the zoo and the occasional sushi or taco date with his wife. With the help of historians and martial artists, PC tries to blend real historical elements with some great rodent action in his stories. Tune in to the Radio Freewrite podcast every Friday to hear original works by PC. Visit PC's website at authorpcnottingham.com and sign up for the newsletter for updates and exclusive content!

Discover more at
4HorsemenPublications.com

10% off using HORSEMEN10